I0533407

The
GOLDEN
CHAIN

E.V. McCall

Copyright © 2024 by E.V. McCall

All rights reserved. No part of this publication may be reproduced, stored or transmitted in any form or by any means, electronic, mechanical, photocopying, recording, scanning, or otherwise without written permission from the publisher. It is illegal to copy this book, post it to a website, or distribute it by any other means without permission.

This novel is entirely a work of fiction. The names, characters and incidents portrayed in it are the work of the author's imagination. Any resemblance to actual persons, living or dead, events or localities is entirely coincidental.

E.V. McCall asserts the moral right to be identified as the author of this work.

First edition

This book was professionally typeset on Reedsy.

Find out more at reedsy.com

Special thanks to Jill, Abby, Stacie, and Mom.

Contents

Pronunciation Guide

Names:

Gwynedd: GWEN-id

Bindor: BEND-or

Gerallt: Jair-ALT

Donan: DO-nehn

Arvel: AR-vuhl

Sinead: SHE-nay-eed

Eamon: EE-uh-monn

Darragh: DA-ra

Bearach: Bare-OCK

Faolan: FOUL-ahn

Lochlann: LOCK-lan

Calev: KAH-lehv

Ciara: KEE-ar-uh

Betrys: BEE-triss

Jeston: JEST-un

Einion: AY-nee-on

Siarl: See-ARL

Gethin: GETH-in

Enid: EE-nid

Torin: TORR-in

Tain: TANE

Mailana: Mail-AH-nuh

Oisin: Oh-SHEEN

Mael: MAIL

Naal: NAIL

Innis: IN-iss

Grathon: Grath-ONN

Padric: PAD-ric

Huilon: HUE-lonn

Ingred: ING-rid

Things & Places:

Acorra: Uh-CORR-uh

Darmor: DAR-more

Ceirian: SARE-ee-ehn

Linlon: LIN-lon

Simlis: SIM-liss

Misituni: Miss-i-toon-ee

Cormos: CORE-mos

Drokond: DRO-kond

Wikanikon: Wick-AH-nick-on

Chapter I

The girl knelt upon the doorstep with her head in her hands until she heard the low thundering of hooves in the northeast. She looked up with widening eyes—lone travelers never came from the forest Darmor, its gray northern borders, or the eastern lands beyond it. Leaping to her feet, she pulled her hair away from her face. In less than a moment, the rider was an arm's length from her.

"What errand could you have—" she began.

"I am not permitted to say," he said. He thrust a piece of parchment into her hands and wheeled away before she could even glimpse his face. Her breath began to come in short, trembling gasps; the message was sealed with a lump of melted gold, and an opal was pressed into it. She hesitated for half a moment and then tore it open.

To the Lady Gwynedd, from a companion and close kinsman of your late father, it read, *I have received news of the unexpected death of your mother's sister. Though I express deep condolences, I fear that you will have no time to grieve. Word has been sent to me that your home will soon be taken by the ruler of the province you inhabit, and thus I urge you to journey east. When you have passed through the Glade of Veilchen, one of the Glade-villagers shall lead you to my palace. I implore you by all*

*you hold dear, do not tell your errand to any among the Wood-people. I am your
servant, Bindor the Bold.*

Gwynedd looked south toward the village and saw horsemen in a cloud of
dust.

She dashed into the house and snatched her cloak, her bow, and her quiver.
"The words of the stranger are fulfilled already," she gasped, rushing to fetch
her horse. The hoofbeats of the villagers' mounts approached as slowly and
steadily as thunder. As they came to the front of the house, they did not see
the edge of Gwynedd's skirt flicker in the wind as she disappeared into the
forest. Almost no light came through the branches of the old, vine covered
trees, and Gwynedd shivered.

The horse, too, was uneasy; it had never been away from the sunny streets
and fields of the village. Gwynedd was nonetheless pleased that she had
escaped the villagers, and she nudged the mare's sides until she began to trot.
The damp leaves made only a soft rustling. They traveled for a day without
incident. By that time the edge of the forest was within sight, and the girl
blinked in the light. It glittered a pale gray. She urged her mare to canter, her
eyes wide. As she passed Darmor's eastern border, her hands began to feel
like ice.

In all her life, Gwynedd had never seen such a thing. The light was as golden
as any other sunlight, but the trees gave it a silver glow. Their bark looked like
a frozen pond, smooth and dark; their leaves were a pale yellow color, like
gold melded with silver. The girl roused herself after a moment and rode on.
After what seemed only a blink of an eye, it was night, but Gwynedd was not
afraid. She slid down from the mare's back and stretched out on the grass.
It was far longer and softer than the grass outside—was, in fact, the loveliest
thing Gwynedd had ever felt. For a few hours, she slept undisturbed. Then,
half-waking, she heard the sound of low, sad singing and struggled to sit
up, shivering violently in the moonlight. She saw a fire being kindled and

bursting into flame in the forest to her left, and, leaving her mare, she rose and began to go towards it.

Behind her she heard a soft *twang*, and she whirled in horror. She saw the metal arrowhead gleaming, but she could not move. Trembling, she shook herself out of her shock and began to run too late. She cried out as it struck her right arm. However, the pain infuriated her, and she fled east before the archer could pursue her. She had never been past Darmor, but she was sure that the Glade-village must be near. It was not. Fortunately, she soon came upon a lone cottage and, finally exhausted, dropped to her knees and crawled through the door.

An old woman rose from a pallet in the corner and hobbled over to the shaking girl. "Who are you?" she said.

"I am Gwynedd," the girl gasped, holding her arm. "Please, good lady, my-my-" She bent toward the floor and shuddered, feeling nauseous.

"Quiet now, child," the lady replied. "I will tend to your wound."

When Gwynedd awoke again, it was daylight. She was lying under a window with the sun upon her face, and, despite her throbbing arm, the archer in the forest seemed no more real than a nightmare.

"May I leave?" she said, sitting up.

The old woman looked at her. "I cannot keep you here, child, but I wish you would have a bit of bread and a drink before you go. I hate to see a little thing like yourself so big-eyed and hungry-looking. And I am frightened; why were you alone in this forest at night?"

The girl shuffled towards the table. "I hope that I may pass the border of the wood before nightfall, if that will ease your mind, good lady. I was unable to stay in my village after my aunt's death. I received a message requesting that I come to a place near the Glade-village, then go to meet a kinsman of my father."

"Very well. Such happenings are common enough. Beg your pardon, child, but what happened to your arm at such an hour?"

"I hardly know, ma'am. I was awakened in the night by voices and the light of a fire. I was cold and hungry and had seen no one for a day, so I rose and went to find where it had come from. I know now that this was foolish, but even so I do not know why the archer wounded me. He was not one of the people who were singing; that I know."

After swallowing a chunk of bread, Gwynedd asked slowly, "Have you any idea who the singers were?"

"I should think you would be more curious about the archer," the woman said, "but if those you heard singing *are* who I daresay they are, I am not surprised at your asking."

Gwynedd leaned against the table and waited, crossing and uncrossing her ankles.

"There are few people who have journeyed through this wood, and fewer still have come here to settle. After a plague in the autumn of last year, only the Wood-people, a band of outlaws, and myself have tarried more than a day among the ceirian-trees."

"Though I do not think you more wise than other girls who have never left their village–I beg your pardon, child, but I fear what might become of you if you do not think seriously– I doubt that you would have run toward the carousing noise of outlaws. What is more, they would have been raucous enough for their song to reach my ears."

"I thought the Silver Wood was great, and spanned many miles," Gwynedd interrupted. "And I certainly feel that I ran a great distance in the night."

"So it is, and I daresay you did, but sounds carry strangely within the forest's borders. That is why fearsome tales have been told concerning it and its people."

"Ah, yes!" Gwynedd said. "Tell me of the people; I had nearly forgotten what I asked of you. I wondered what the tales might be and forgot the more crucial matters at hand."

"Your village has changed greatly since I left it, if you have forgotten the tales of the Silver Wood," the old woman said, sighing. "No matter. I must tell you one thing that is more vital than all else: the Wood-people are the only folk east of Darmor and west of the Glade-village that are entirely safe. It would ease my mind if you were going to their lands instead of the eastern coast."

"Should I be?" Gwynedd said.

The woman looked up. "I do not fully know your errand, and I will not counsel you, but they say that the outlaws come from caves near the sea."

The girl narrowed her eyes. "These outlaws– who are they loyal to?"

"Some claim to be led by a man named Bindor, who is a great lord and wields much power over all of Acorra. His brother was named Gerallt; he called himself King of Acorra and was a good and true man, though deceived by Bindor. Acorra's king ought to be a man among the Wood-folk– but I will not speak of him to you. He does not wish yet to claim his place or confront Bindor, though I know not why."

"This Gerallt," Gwynedd said, staring into her cup and tapping her fingers against it, "what became of him?"

"He was slain many years ago by a party of Wood-folk while he was hunting in their lands. The men were punished severely–I have heard, though I doubt the truth of it, that two were killed– for they had been forbidden to lay a hand on Gerallt, Bindor, or any of their people." Gwynedd rose and nodded.

"I thank you for your courtesy," she said, turning toward the door.

"Do not journey far until your arm is better healed," the old woman said.

Gwynedd smiled. "I will not."

Then she shut the door and exhaled. She set her face eastward and began to walk, feeling the loss of her mare keenly. She had worked in the small garden and ridden to the village many times when she had lived with her aunt, but she had never been allowed to walk anywhere alone, and her aunt had been too weak to leave the cottage for years.

Thus, the girl found the rolling ground profoundly difficult, and she almost struggled to draw breath. She never guessed that the old woman had been in earnest, and that her wound had taken a great toll on her strength. Not until she knelt by a stream and reached her hand down to get a drink did she recall the warning. A keen throb in her shoulder made her cry out in shock.

"Ah!" she said. Then the crackling of leaves on the other side of the water silenced her. Trembling, she lifted a sharp stone from the stream and struggled to her feet. As she did so, three brown-clad archers stepped out from the shadows of the trees. "Lay the stone down, my lady," the tallest said. She looked carefully at his face as she put the rock on the grass. He seemed quite grave, and neither his sternness nor that of his companions was lessened when Gwynedd stretched out her empty hands.

"What have I done?" she said.

"You have done nothing deserving of reproach, but we must take you to our prince nevertheless. The greatest fear of all his court is a prying enemy roaming his lands."

As the men crossed the stream and bound her wrists, Gwynedd said, "What has caused this fear to come into your prince's heart?"

The men laughed. "To our chagrin, Prince Arvel does not fear the couriers of his enemies. It is left to us to remind him that all our folk are in danger even now. If our present state were discovered by a messenger of Bindor, our peril would be increased a thousandfold."

Gwynedd nodded, then brooded wearily until her captors began to slow their pace. Then she roused herself and looked about. It appeared that they had reached the Wood-folk's village, and it was a strange sight to Gwynedd.

The houses, which rose up on either side of the grassy street, were built of white river-stones. Golden flowers twined about the walls and fluttered in the warm breeze. Gwynedd, used to Darmor-village, with its shabby, straw-thatched wooden houses, inhaled sharply at the sight.

"When you see the house of Arvel, you will gasp indeed," the guards laughed. They led her toward the tallest home, which was at the end of the long lane. She was nearly too frightened to inhale, much less gasp, when she stood before the great doors. Her captors released her arms and knocked, and two guards flung the gates wide.

The tall archer walked with Gwynedd, directing her down two halls and a flight of stairs into a bright room with blue carpets thrown over the gray floor. The wall that looked out toward the trees was made almost entirely of glass. In front of it, a young man sat on an oaken throne. He was gripping the arms of his seat and his eyes were downcast, but he rose swiftly and looked at Gwynedd when she halted before him. Nodding to the soldier, he said, "Donan, who is this?"

"We found the girl at the east stream," the soldier said.

Arvel nodded, his eyebrows lowering from their raised position, and turned to Gwynedd. "I trust that my soldiers have treated you fairly, my lady?" His voice was deep and quiet, and his eyes were grave.

He was quite unlike the noisy merchants of Gwynedd's acquaintance, and she took care to answer him graciously. "I found nothing to complain of in their conduct, Your Grace."

"Excellent. That is as it should be." His eyes fell upon her blood-stained sleeve, then flashed at his servant. "I hope that this woman was not injured by one of my people, for if she was—"

"No, no, Your Grace," the soldier stammered.

"Very well. Has her wound been attended to, Donan?"

"No, Your Grace," Donan said.

"Then I must do it myself before I question her any further," the prince said. "She should not be made to speak more in this condition. Fetch my sister to assist me."

Gwynedd stepped forward, her eyes widening. "Your Grace, begging your pardon, I am not—"

He held up his hand and silenced her. Arvel's sister soon returned with Donan. After gently pulling up Gwynedd's loose sleeve, she shook her head.

"It is deep and beyond my little skill, though it is not mortal." Gwynedd went white.

"Fear not," Arvel said. Turning to his sister, he asked, "Did you bring the ceirian-bark and linlon-petals?" She nodded and spread the contents of her satchel out on the floor. Arvel knelt and gathered what he needed. "Sit upon the carpet," he told Gwynedd. His sister held up the girl's sleeve as he slathered the poultice on her forearm and wrapped a long bandage around it. It burned more sharply than flaming coals against her skin, but she was too awed and exhausted to make any noise.

When Arvel had finished, he helped Gwynedd to her feet and then said to his sister, "Have you some place in your home where she might stay the night?"

Sinead nodded briefly. "Yes."

"Excellent," Arvel said. "You may lead her there now, for she is weary; I will question her at daybreak."

"But—" his sister protested.

"She can do no harm in your house, Sinead. I will question her at the moment the sun rises. Already the night grows old; she will be in your care for almost no time."

"Yes, brother," Sinead said, sighing quietly. She grasped Gwynedd's wrist and led her out of the house.

"Your brother does not often send prisoners to your home, surely?" Gwynedd asked.

"No;" Sinead replied, "you are the first woman he has ever had need to question. I am glad and surprised that he is questioning you at all."

"So you think him too lenient in his dealings with enemies?" Gwynedd said.

"I—" Sinead began. Then she pursed her lips. "'Twould be wrong to discuss such things with a captive," she said. She led Gwynedd into her house. Releasing Gwynedd's wrist, she pointed to a corner. "You may sleep there. I will find you a blanket," Sinead said. Though Gwynedd had not eaten since the early morning, her heavy head and eyelids overcame her hunger and she fell asleep swiftly on the cold floor.

At dawn, Sinead shook her prisoner's shoulders and whispered, "Hurry! My brother is waiting!"

Gwynedd gasped and leapt to her feet. "I am sorry," she replied.

Sinead watched the girl pick up her cloak and then sighed. "Stop. I cannot take you to my brother in that state; he will have my head. Follow me." Sinead led Gwynedd through a long hall into a little room and sat her on a stool. After handing her a green dress, she combed her hair and led her back outside. When they reached the steps leading to Arvel's throne room, Sinead said,

"I am not permitted to come with you. Farewell."

"Thank you," Gwynedd replied. As she descended the stairs, she raised her eyes slowly to Arvel's face.

"Welcome," the prince said. He motioned to a chair that faced his throne, and Gwynedd lowered herself gingerly into it.

"I know you do not wish to be in my lands, and I will neither keep you here long nor question you deeply," he said.

"I am at your service, Your Grace," she said.

"I thank you. What is your name, and where have you come from?"

"I am Gwynedd. I come from the village on the outskirts of Darmor."

Arvel looked at his hands, his brow furrowed. "Gwynedd. Only once before have I heard that name, but it did not belong to a maiden of Darmor."

Gwynedd stared at her boots and said slowly, "I have not always lived near Darmor. My parents did not come from there."

"In what land did they dwell?"

"I know nothing of the place, save that it was east of the dark forest. And it was neither in your lands nor in the Glade-village."

"What was your father called?" Arvel said. His eyes were brightening, though his face was graver than before. Gwynedd turned away and stared at the wall.

The prince rose and looked at her. "Lady Gwynedd, I cannot release you when you have told me so little. My people will not allow it, and even if it did not irk them, I fear that you may endanger us. Tell me the name of your father."

"Your Grace, I cannot. You will never allow me to leave your lands, even if you are merciful enough to leave me alive. I beg of you, do not force me. Do not torture me. I will tell you anything but the name of my father."

"On my honor, my lady," Arvel replied, "if your father was Bindor himself, I will do nothing to you."

Gwynedd, her face as pale as death, relented. "He was Gerallt," she whispered.

Chapter II

Arvel clenched his teeth and nodded slowly. "Very well," he replied. He motioned for Gwynedd to rise and said, "I will not turn back on my word. You do not have to remain in my land. However, I beg you, do not reveal how little my strength is. Bindor does not know the toll last year's plague took upon my people. Farewell, if you choose to journey on; welcome, if you choose to tarry."

"Farewell, Your Grace," Gwynedd said in a low voice, wobbling slightly as she tried to curtsy.

"There is no enmity between us, Gwynedd, because of your father." Arvel said, stepping toward the girl as she turned away. "Your fate lies in your own hands."

She stared at him. "I do not understand, Your Grace."

"You understand, my lady. Perhaps you wonder how I know your intentions, but you understand my meaning."

Gwynedd stepped forward and furrowed her brow. "Sir, how could you know?"

"I do not know the very place; I only guess. But this I know: you did not wish to come to my lands, and neither do you wish to remain here. Your sympathies do not lie with me."

"I hardly know you," she protested.

"Neither do you know Lord Bindor. You have chosen his side because the benefit to yourself will be greater, or so you think."

"I have not chosen Lord Bindor's side," she snapped.

"But you have not chosen mine," Arvel said quietly.

"You cannot keep me here and speak to me in this way, Your Grace, although I am your lesser," Gwynedd said, looking away. "I have done nothing wrong."

"Neither have I tried to do so," he said. "Go, if it is your wish."

She turned and climbed the steps without looking back and ran through the halls into the courtyard. "Please, allow me to go through the gates," she asked the guards. They hesitated. "Lord Arvel said that I may journey on from his realm if I wish it, sir," Gwynedd begged the older guard. She saw that the man was staring back towards the door, and she turned to look. Arvel stood in the doorway to the courtyard.

"Let her go," he said.

Gwynedd went through the gates with her eyes on the ground. The street was empty and unwatched, and her footfalls seemed noisy as she padded over the grass. She had nearly reached the end of the path when she heard something on her left. Confused, she listened for a moment before looking around the end of the last house. There were three rows of homes stretching down to the banks of the stream, and three men stood in front of one of them. Gwynedd stepped nearer and heard what they were saying.

"Have you any guess where she came from?" a peasant asked a man who appeared to be a soldier.

"Not in the slightest. She is not one of the outlaw's animals, that is clear. You can scarcely see those beasts through the jewels encrusting them, and this mare has no saddle and merely a plain bridle. She galloped up from the west, but you know how animals wander about. I suppose I will take her to Arvel."

Gwynedd had heard enough. She stepped around the corner of the house and descended the hill. "Perchance you are discussing a bright bay mare with a white patch on her muzzle and one white foreleg on the off-side, with a small scar on the near side of her chest?"

The soldier started. "The animal is like your words in every way, but how would you know of her?"

"I believe that she is mine. I have traveled here from Darmor-village, and I lost my horse when I was injured three nights ago."

The man furrowed his brow. "Though I do not doubt your truthfulness, I must still show the animal to the prince, and you must present your case before him."

Gwynedd looked down, biting her lip. "I have already spoken with your prince," she replied shortly.

"About your horse?" the soldier asked.

"No," she replied, "but nonetheless, he said that I am permitted to leave his lands. The animal does not belong to any of your people, and thus, even if I were stealing it, the matter does not concern you. You have no reason to detain me here."

The man shook his head. "You do not understand our law. If a person or animal strays into Arvel's land, they must remain there until the prince allows their departure. It is one of the few rights he retains. All consider it a just law–aside from the people of Bindor, and they are exempted to avoid conflict. Our prince asks little, considering what should rightfully be his."

Gwynedd bit her lip. It did not seem prudent to reveal that she was Lord Bindor's niece, even had she been resolved to side with her uncle; and as it was, she was not yet sure if that was preferable to humoring Arvel. So she finally sighed. "Very well," she said.

One of the other peasants went to fetch the mare, and when the animal was handed to the soldier, he motioned for Gwynedd to follow him. The girl felt that if she was forced to tread the long path to Arvel's palace once more, she would leave mare, cloak, and shoes behind to avoid it. This time the gates were open, and the prince stood under the archway speaking with a guard. He raised an eyebrow when he saw Gwynedd, and the soldier rushed to explain his, the mare's, and the girl's presence.

"I saw this mare drinking at the stream near my home early this morning. When I was discussing the matter with two farmers a few moments ago, this young woman appeared and described the mare exactly. She insists that the animal belongs to her."

"Very well," Arvel said. "If the mare is hers–and I daresay it is– then we must give it to her; and if it is not, it is not my place to judge her crime in my lands."

Gwynedd smiled and began to reach for her mare's reins, but the guard Arvel had been speaking to frowned and said, "Should a woman of her lineage and loyalties be allowed to leave with a mare that is not only swift, but also, by all appearances, valiant–an animal that could be put to good use in battle?" His voice was low, but Gwynedd heard every word. She looked Arvel in the eyes.

He gazed back quietly, shaking his head. There was no submissiveness in Gwynedd's face even yet. "You are right; it is not wise to do so," he said, "and so I will give her two choices. Lady Gwynedd, you may either depart to whatever part of Acorra that you please without your horse or take the mare and vow, on your honor, that you will not travel to join Bindor."

Gwynedd clasped her hands behind her back and shifted her weight, then said, "Am I permitted to remain in your lands?"

Arvel's eyes widened. "Why do you wish to remain here?"

"I do not have the strength, Your Grace, to travel without my mare, and although I may not purpose to join the ranks of your enemy, I feel that it is unjust for you to prevent me from doing so. I would be of no use to Bindor. Thus, I wish to remain here so that my health is not lost and so that I am not forced to comply with your restrictions on my wanderings."

Arvel nodded. "You may remain here as long as you wish," he replied, "but I beg you, if your intentions in remaining are other than those you have told me, forsake them."

She nodded and began to turn away, but he stepped forward and said in a lower voice, "Do not disregard the trust I have given to you. You know the perilous place my people have found themselves in."

Gwynedd looked down at the reins in her hands. "As I have told you, Your Grace, my importance is far smaller than you guess."

"So you think," he said. He stepped back and nodded at her gravely, and she walked away after curtsying. When she reached the end of the village, she pulled herself onto her mare (with some difficulty; her arm still pained her) and rode southwest towards the stream. She took care not to stray far from the village, for she feared the archer who had wounded her, but she did not want to be on the very outskirts of town like some wretched beggar.

There was no doubt in Gwynedd's mind as to what she would do when morning came. She was unwatched and trusted; there was nothing to stand in the way of her fleeing. However, she began to feel that waiting until dawn was foolish.

"I will sleep only an hour," she said to herself. When she woke again, it seemed as bright as day, and she struggled to her feet in a panic.

"Only the moonlight," she exhaled. The golden trees, which had seemed to close in a bright cage around her, allowed her to breathe again. She wished, nonetheless, that the moon was not full. There were no clouds near it; she could not hope that it would be covered soon. Her only hope lay in utter silence. Finding a sharp stone, she tore strips from her cloak to quiet the pounding of her mare's hooves. The dress she wore was thicker and would have served better, but Gwynedd was unwilling to mutilate as well as steal Sinead's gown. After she had wrapped the cloth around the horse's hooves, there were no other precautions that could be taken. She grasped the animal's rough mane and dragged herself up. She looked up at the cold stars to be comforted by their soft light, then nudged the horse and rode on.

Gwynedd had intended to cross in front of Arvel's palace, ride north a short way, and then journey east, but she had not expected for the great house to be guarded on all sides. When she turned the corner and saw the moonlight glinting on the soldier's helmets, she wheeled around and rode down the south wall.

At the end of the wall, she halted and shivered. Someone was in the courtyard.

"She does not know that she is of any value to him," the voice said. Gwynedd knew after two words that it was Arvel.

"Then why do you fear?" a voice that Gwynedd did not know asked.

"I have no doubt that she believes, nonetheless, that she will be better off in his lands. It may very well be true; if she remains here, he may receive word of it, attack us, and take her."

"Then you intend to send her away?"

There was a silence that lasted several moments before Arvel replied, "No. I hope to convince her to allow me to regain the kingship of Acorra, for if I can do so, all Bindor's hope is lost. My guards have reported that his people grow impatient—"

Gwynedd kicked her mare suddenly. She had a suspicion that the conversation would soon be over, and if Arvel returned to his throne room, he would be in front of the glass wall; her way of escape would be watched. The mare traveled at a jerky trot over the riverbank in front of the glass wall. Then she wheeled and rode past the side of the village at a canter.

After she was out of the sight of even a far-wandering guard, Gwynedd's breath came more easily. For an hour the ride was a pleasure; the moon shone, and the mare went smoothly and swiftly over the even ground. When the sky became covered over with clouds, however, Gwynedd's head began to ache from squinting. The trees cast strange shadows on her path. The mare was tiring, and her rider was forced to slow her to a walk.

This was a bitter blow to Gwynedd, who had wished fervently that she might reach some place of shelter before dawn. She was afraid that she could not think clearly enough to ride all night, but it could not be helped. Nothing could induce her to sleep in the Silver Wood. So she clenched her teeth, feeling sick with weariness, and entwined her hands in the mare's mane to hold herself steady if she happened to slip. When the sun's earliest rays began to fall on the roofs of the Glade-village houses, Gwynedd saw them for the first time.

Her horse's hooves crunched on leaves for one last stride, then squished on damp grass. As soon as the mare stepped into the clearing in the midst of the houses, Gwynedd slid down and let out a long breath. To her chagrin, there seemed to be no more chance for lodging here than there had been in the forest. Every house's windows were shuttered and every door was barred. Not wishing to be thought a beggar or a madwoman, she wandered back out of the village. Driving a branch into the ground, she tethered her mare and laid down in the grass.

The burning sun on Gwynedd's face and the sound of shouting awakened her. She leapt to her feet. When she saw the villagers beginning to approach her, she rushed to untether her horse and leapt onto its back. However, she knew that she would be pursued if she tried to flee, so she rode slowly up to the crowd.

"Greetings," she said.

"Who are you, and what might your business in our lands be?" a farmer demanded.

"I am Gwynedd," she said. After a moment of hesitation, she remembered the letter she had received and added,

"I am the daughter of Gerallt, and I was summoned by a man who calls himself Bindor the Bold. Might you tell me where I may join him?"

The entire crowd stepped back. "You are the daughter of Gerallt, King of Acorra?" the farmer whispered.

"Unless I am gravely mistaken, sir," Gwynedd said, flushing slightly.

"The man you wish to find dwells to the east of our village. There is a young man who lives among us who has also been summoned by Bindor, and he will accompany you to the place."

"Thank you," Gwynedd said. "May I ask for a morsel of food and a cup of water before I journey on?"

Another man, far more richly dressed than the farmer, stepped out of the crowd. "Our best is too poor for you, Princess. As it is my son who has been summoned, I beg you to eat what meager fare my wife and I can provide before Eamon takes you to Bindor."

Gwynedd slipped down from her mare's back. "I am unutterably grateful, good sir. My horse—"

"I will tend to the animal," a little boy said, endeavoring to look very willing and eager (his mother had just poked him firmly).

"Thank you," the princess said.

After having far more food and drink thrust upon her than she had desired, Gwynedd's mare was returned to her, and she set out with her host's son, Eamon.

"I have heard many tales of Gerallt," he said as they rode east over the green fields, "but I would not shun hearing more. What was he like, my lady?"

The girl looked down. "I did not know him," she said, "but my aunt, my mother's sister who raised me, told me a little of him."

"I should like to hear, if it would not trouble you," the boy said.

"Very well. I know nothing of his looks, but I suppose his hair must have been dark, and I think that he was tall. My mother was small and golden-haired, and of course I do not look like her."

"No," Eamon said politely.

"As for his character, I have heard much, but my aunt cared nothing for him. Thus, what you have heard is doubtlessly more truthful."

"Perhaps," he said.

Gwynedd gave him a sideways glance. "She said that he was courageous and kind, but became cold and arrogant after a time. He met my mother in some village marketplace and helped her carry her goods home in the rain, though even then he was a great man and she was only a peasant. And for years, aunt said, all was well; after that she would tell me little more. What she told me I do not care to say."

Eamon nodded slowly.

"Did she speak the truth?" Gwynedd said.

Her companion looked down. "All that she said was truthful, but I do not wish to tell you more either. I would make myself susceptible to any of the cruelest punishments."

"Speak," she said. "I demand it." Her face had grown pale, and there was fear behind the anger in her eyes.

"It is said that Gerallt and Bindor began to cross the borders of the Silver Wood at their leisure, and it was their most grievous wrong. Darragh, who had once called himself King, retained the rule of that wood, and he had begged Gerallt's people not to cross its borders unless their errand was dire—he knew that otherwise, all his strength would be lost. On one cold day in early spring, a score of years ago, Gerallt rode over the border alone and never returned. Though it was said Darragh did not order the death of his enemy, Bindor sent a soldier to assassinate the Wood-king."

"I have one thing and one only to say; your village should be called gibberish, not glade, for it seems that idle gossip is your greatest skill. Never have I heard even the name of Darragh, and though I know my father became unkind, he was always a man of his word."

Eamon looked at her and squared his jaw. "It is not mentioned, either by his folk or ours, in idle chatter with strangers, and your village knows almost nothing of it. If you were not the daughter of Gerallt, I would not have told the tale to you either."

Gwynedd turned away for a moment and then said, "I am sorry. But surely you cannot think that Gerallt was wrong in that matter. The wood belonged to him by true right, and not to Darragh."

"I–" the boy said.

"You cannot think that it was Darragh who was the rightful king of Acorra!"

The boy went pallid. "Nay! Nay! The thought never passed through my mind, though I am reckless. I feel only that the matter should have been treated with more delicacy. Darragh was convinced that the right to rule was his. His people still believe this, and that is why Gerallt and Bindor's people treat them cautiously."

Chapter III

"But that is foolish," Gwynedd said. "Why did he believe such a thing?"

Eamon shook his head. "It is a long tale that I cannot tell you here. We will soon reach the castle of Bindor."

"Very well," Gwynedd said. She sighed. "I thank you."

Eamon smiled. "I have done nothing worthy of praise."

The girl shook her head. "Nay. Your tales captivated me, strange though they are."

"Yes. Well, we must speak no more of those matters. You may say what you wish, of course," he said, "but I do not wish to displease Bindor."

"Nay, I will say no more now. I will discuss these matters with my uncle in due time." She looked forward and trembled. They were riding along a gray path that ran beside a dark, swirling river, and a cold wind blew over the green waters. Soon, however, they rode around a bend and saw the castle. It was built of light-colored stones, with towers that reached hundreds of feet into the sky and intricately carven windows.

Gwynedd breathed in the salty breeze and heard the song of the sea for the first time, and her lips parted in a smile. She looked down at the shore-grasses blowing around her mare's legs. Seeing that the ground was already sandy and peppered with white shells, she turned to Eamon and said, "Surely the castle is not built on the shore itself?"

"No," Eamon said. "There is a great stone under it, a stone that was left when a cliff collapsed long ago. Do you not see how much higher it is than the ground around it?"

"Now I see," Gwynedd said.

After a few moments she heard Eamon say, "My lady?"

Gwynedd turned her head. "Yes?"

"I asked if you once lived in the palace."

"I do not think so," she said. Her voice was flat, and she was looking off toward the sea. Then she turned to Eamon and smiled, pointing towards the shore.

"I must see it," she said.

The boy shrugged good-naturedly. "I must report to Bindor, but you are Gerallt's daughter. Do as you like." He smiled and gestured east. "Go on," he said.

She spun the mare around and trotted downhill through the marshy grasses. When she reached the smooth, wide sands, she urged her mare to canter. The sand was deep, and the mare slowed and stopped after twenty paces, but Gwynedd did not notice. She had reached the edge of the water, and she threw herself down from the horse's bare back. The bright, cool seawater caressed her ankles and dampened the edge of her skirt. As she stared at the foamy waves, her attention was diverted by a sudden movement on the palace balcony.

She saw a tall, dark-haired man leaning against the marble railing of the platform. The palace was not close enough for her to determine much about his face, but it seemed stern and grave. Gwynedd felt at once that she should not have come to amuse herself in the waves before going to meet her uncle, and she pulled herself back onto her mare. There did not seem to be a door below the balcony, so she rode past the watching man and went to the front gates of the castle. When the gates were flung open, she said, "I am Gwynedd, daughter of Gerallt."

"My lady," the guards replied simultaneously. They bowed for a moment and then the one who stood on the right turned to cry, "Bearach! A great lady requires her mare to be stabled. Tell Faolan to make the straw deep in the corner stall, and you come fetch the animal."

"Yes, father!" a small voice said. A red-headed boy came around the corner and took the mare's reins after bowing to Gwynedd. The horse, who was not used to strangers, arched her neck and snorted, but she walked along obediently.

Bearach's father tarried a moment to see that his son took the mare to the stable and then turned to Gwynedd. "I am Captain Lochlann; if it pleases you, my lady, I will take you to Bindor," he said.

Gwynedd nodded. "Thank you." As she followed Lochlann, she looked regretfully at her sandy skirt and frayed cloak. *'Tis hardly befitting for a queen to come to her castle in such a state,* she thought. But she forgot her appearance (and all else about herself) when they entered the palace. The high, arching ceiling, which seemed as infinite as the sky, was painted the purest white she had ever seen. Lochlann went before her on a spiraling staircase that led into a bright room looking out over the sea. Gwynedd noticed that the now-empty balcony was connected to the room, and she looked around for the dark-haired man.

"Greetings, Lady Gwynedd," a deep voice to her right said. She whirled and saw him on a tall gray throne.

"I am Bindor," he said.

Gwynedd curtsied deeply. "Greetings, my uncle," she said. "I apologize for not coming to meet you more promptly."

"Were you detained on your journey?" he said. He leaned forward, his brow furrowing.

"Only slightly," she said. "I was referring to my tarrying at the shore. The delay on my journey was insignificant." She was unwilling to tell Bindor either of the hindrances she had encountered.

"I cherish no bitterness against you for wishing to see the great ocean," Bindor said, smiling. "I could not have expected my brother's child to act otherwise. Your father also loved the sea."

Gwynedd smiled.

"And even if you had acted discourteously, the fault would be mine. I should have sent for you sooner and raised you in circumstances that befitted your lineage, but I did not wish to offend your mother's sister. She cherished no affection toward your father and I. Do not mistake me, of course," he said, "I was not bitter towards her."

"I believe you, good uncle," Gwynedd said.

Bindor smiled. "I see that the gentleness of your manners could hardly have been improved by a more noble upbringing. You are very like my brother." He looked down for a moment, but raised his eyes quickly. "I will waste no time in declaring you Queen of Acorra. The people will not be displeased, for they have been waiting long for Gerallt's daughter to sit upon the Throne of Calev."

"If it does not displease your lordship," Gwynedd said, "I desire to learn the laws of Acorra more thoroughly and speak with the barons of the land before I assume the throne."

He nodded. "I see that you are a wise lady," he said. "But matters of state may wait until tomorrow. I see that you are weary and hungry from your long journey. I offer my sincerest apologies for making you travel without an escort, but I cannot send horsemen through the Silver Wood, and I could not let a lady travel along the northern path that avoids the wood. It is a perilous and lonely way."

"Your apologies are not required," Gwynedd said. "My journey was not unpleasant."

"That is well," Bindor said, "but I will, nonetheless, summon servants to assist you in bathing and finding fitting garments, and then you may come to a feast I will order prepared." He rose from his seat and clapped his hands. Two guards at the other end of the room disappeared through a marble door and reappeared with two fair-haired maidens clad in gowns of soft blue.

After the men reassumed their posts by the door, the girls came forward and curtsied to Gwynedd. "I am Ciara, and with me is my sister Betrys," she said. "We will lead you to the chambers that were prepared for you."

Gwynedd gave a grave nod and smiled, then followed the maidens down the staircase she had ascended a few minutes earlier. They led her down a long hall with many windows into a doorway on the right. She caught her breath. The room was beautiful, to be sure, but the things that caught her attention were the golden flowers painted on the walls. *They are linlon-flowers,* she thought. *Perhaps the Wood-king Darragh dwelt both by the sea and in the woodlands before he–before his crown was given to my father.* Then she saw Ciara staring at her.

"I beg your pardon," Gwynedd said.

"Nay, Your Grace," the maid said. "I will not reproach you. I merely said that you may choose any gown you wish from the white trunk by the window, and my sister and I will press it for you while you bathe."

"Thank you," Gwynedd said.

After Ciara had laid a sea-green gown on the bed, she said, "I will undress you." She pulled down Gwynedd's right sleeve and then stopped. For a long moment, she was silent.

The young queen turned to face the maid and flushed as she pulled her sleeve back up. "It is nothing. I was wounded slightly on my journey."

Ciara pulled the sleeve down again, and Gwynedd was afraid to stop her when she began to unwind the bandage. "It is dressed with gray bark and golden flowers," Ciara said. Her voice was very low, and Gwynedd saw her cross her arms.

Gwynedd knew that if she did not give Ciara any explanation, disaster would result. It was impossible to know what conclusions the girl would draw if she was not given part of the truth. "I was wounded by a vagabond archer," Gwynedd said. "The wound is insignificant. An old woman, who lives alone in the Silver Wood, dressed it for me."

Ciara nodded. "I have seen her home, and all who live between Darmor and the sea know that she can no longer travel farther than a mile from her cottage. She grows no golden flowers, nor do they grow near her home. It was only two months before today when I left Darmor-village with my brother and passed the cottage. I saw all the lands around it."

"I crossed to the realm beyond the stream. The golden flowers grow there."

"Very well; but you did not tend to the wound on your own right arm," Ciara said.

"Nay, I did not. But—"

Betrys came out from behind the white curtain that separated the bathtub from the rest of the room, balancing a jug on her hip, and said, "The bath is full and warm, Your Grace."

"Thank you," Gwynedd said. She looked at Ciara and said in a low voice,

"Do not be concerned over this matter. I will speak of all important subjects to my uncle tomorrow, as we have already decided."

The servant opened her mouth, but swiftly closed it and nodded obediently as she curtsied. Betrys picked up the gown on the bed, curtsied to Gwynedd, and followed her sister, shutting the door behind both of them.

After she had bathed, slipped into the linen gown, and gone to the meal with her uncle, Gwynedd was tired but restless. She slipped down the hall and out the gate; the guards let her out without requiring any explanation. Turning east, she walked past the north wall of the palace and out onto the sand. Then she stopped. Her boots, which she had found in the trunk with the gown, were too soft and clean to wear in the sand and saltwater. She slipped them off and threw them in the rough grass, then wandered back to the water's edge. As she watched the clear waves lap around her ankles, she heard a crunching noise behind her and turned to see her uncle coming down the sloping shore.

He smiled gravely. "Though I said we would not discuss matters of state until the morrow, it seems that you are refreshed," he said, "and I thought that I could answer any queries you may have that pertain to small and general matters. I am no great scholar, but I know enough of Acorra to tell you a little."

After looking down for a moment, he added very slowly, "And I wish to know if what your servant told me is truthful—that you encountered Wood-folk on your journey."

Gwynedd jerked her head up, her cheeks flushed and her eyes widening. "I–"

"You do not need to defend yourself," Bindor said. "I trust my brother's daughter far more than I trust the servants of my household. I will not judge your actions until I have heard the true tale of them."

Gwynedd felt sick. She swallowed and then began to speak. "On the first night I spent in the Silver Wood, I awoke to the sound of strange and beautiful singing. I saw a fire flickering through the trees; I wondered who the mysterious people might be, and I was hungry and cold. The fire seemed great and warm, and I did not think that the folk around it were cruel or wild. I arose to find it. In the darkness, I heard a sudden *twang*, and before I could flee, a ragged outlaw's arrow had struck my right arm. Maddened by the pain, I ran to a cottage where an old woman cared for me."

She looked up at her uncle, whose flushed cheeks were stretched tight by his clenched jaw. "Ciara told me of the linlon-flowers," he said.

Gwynedd swallowed again. "I was captured by the Wood-folk. They treated me with the utmost courtesy, uncle. They merely wished to know my errand in their lands."

The flush on Bindor's face was growing. "I hope you told them that you wandered into their lands by chance and had no errand there."

She looked down at the water and listened to its sorrowful crashing for a moment. Then she said, "I told them that I had not come to their lands with any intention to remain there, nor to do them harm. He—they guessed that I was one of your people and was traveling towards your land. I—"

"Surely you did not admit to this accusation!" Bindor said.

Gwynedd looked away again. "No," she repeated, "I did not tell them my errand."

Her uncle snatched her arm. "Did they guess it?"

The color drained from her face so completely that she felt it. "They did not guess my errand," she said, "but they know who I am."

Bindor let go of her arm and was silent for a moment. "Gwynedd, brother's daughter, hope of our kindred, Queen of Acorra, you have gravely endangered us. I have lain low and wielded little of the power I possess over the land, and the people of the wood have given me no trouble. I fear that now, now that they know Gerallt's daughter wishes to claim the throne, they will attack. I desired to keep your presence concealed until we could gather my soldiers and persuade the prince of the Wood-folk to surrender his power."

"For power he has, Gwynedd, and I fear that he may attempt an attack to prevent you from assuming the throne. I said that I wielded little power because I wished to be cautious, but that is not the entire truth. You are the heir of Gerallt. It is you to whom Acorra will rally, if you wish it. I did not possess this power, and the Prince Arvel knows this. He has been waiting for your appearance; though my demise would have made things difficult for you, there would still have been some who would have rallied to you. Now his time is ripe, and our danger is great."

Gwynedd bit her lip. She did not wish to tell her uncle that Arvel had not the strength to attack, for she did not know her uncle's heart. She feared that he might wish to annihilate his rivals even if they posed no immediate threat. Arvel's folk, diminished as he said it was, might nonetheless hide in a corner of Acorra and rise against Bindor's people when the time was truly ripe.

"I do not know what to say to you, my uncle," she said. Lowering her eyes, she looked at the waves. Her stomach felt tight and empty; the little she had eaten at the feast had done her no good.

Bindor let out a long sigh and shook his head. "I will not blame you. As I said, I accept the fault for all of your wrongdoing. Your upbringing was not what it ought to have been. However, I will have my scholars begin to tutor you tomorrow in the ways of our kindred and teach you the greatness of your father. I believe that any matters of state I would have discussed with you pale in importance to this crisis, and thus I shall speak with my army while you pursue your studies. We will endeavor to escape the peril we have become ensnared in."

Gwynedd nodded slowly, swallowing in a vain effort to release the tightness in her throat. "Yes, uncle. I am at your service."

The next day dawned bright and cold. Gwynedd, after dressing quickly, asked her maid to lead her to the library.

"Do you not wish to eat breakfast, Your Grace?" Ciara said.

Gwynedd looked away. "No."

The servant sighed and motioned for Gwynedd to follow her. They reached the wide, wood-paneled room after a long walk down cold and silent hallways.

"I will leave you now," Ciara said, "if you no longer require my services."

"You may go," Gwynedd replied. She slipped through the wide doorway and looked around.

"Greetings," a cheery voice said from somewhere.

Gwynedd's hand flew to her chest. Her breath came more easily when the elderly man, dressed in the plain gray doublet of Acorran scholars, appeared from behind a bookshelf. "Greetings," she said, smiling.

"I am Jeston," the scholar said, "whom some call The Learned, and though I in no way deserve this distinction, I will offer you my humble services in your learning, Your Grace."

"That is kind, grandfather," Gwynedd said.

"I only do my duty," Jeston said, bowing slightly. Then he straightened and squared his shoulders. "This day, we will study the most crucial principles of Acorran law, learn a little of botany and medicine (this only in caution, should Your Grace ever venture to the wilderness and become injured or hungry by some unfortunate happenstance), the lineage of Your Grace's most noble kindred, and the great deeds of Your Grace's illustrious and virtuous father."

"These are indeed worthy subjects," Gwynedd said. After an uncomfortable pause, she continued, for it was clear that Jeston expected her to.

"Might we also speak of the dangers that even now challenge my royal person and my most fair and worthy kingdom? The Silver Wood and its people weigh heavily upon my mind."

Jeston did not look as surprised, nor as offended, as Gwynedd had expected him to look. He nodded gravely and said, "We will speak of it after we discuss Your Grace's lineage and father."

They went to a large table and pulled out two heavy chairs. Six books were spread over the tabletop. The lesson in law was preliminary; Gwynedd knew much of it from hearing tales of criminals in Darmor-village. Botany was equally simple. It was only when Jeston opened the dusty volume that contained the Annals of the Kings of Acorra that a keen light came into her eyes.

Chapter IV

"The line of the Acorran kings," the tutor said, "began in the two-hundredth Year of the Sundering with Calev the Seafarer. His father hailed from Simlis, and it was said that his mother came from the South-lands near Misituni, from the country of the Chosen of God."

Gwynedd looked up. "Not since our hearts were first enlightened with knowledge of the Lord have we heard news from that land, and the Son, the King, lived centuries ago. It is strange that fate took a woman from that realm to the North-lands."

"Indeed," Jeston said, "and this is why men esteemed Calev. He was strong and great, for his father was a hero in Simlis; but he achieved acclaim by his wisdom. His sons had sons for many generations—their names Your Grace may learn on another day, for this day grows old and we have much yet to learn— until, in the eight hundredth Year of the Sundering, a strange thing took place."

"The heir to the throne, Einion the Tall, relinquished his kingship to the son of his cousin, a man named Siarl. Siarl's great-grandson's great-grandson was called Darragh. In the twentieth year of his reign, Darragh went on a voyage to the island of Cormos (Acorra's territory, as you know, since the seven hundredth Year of the Sundering), and left Your Grace's noble father, Gerallt the Valiant, as his regent. Though Gerallt was loyal to Darragh, he was Einion's heir, and it was brought to his attention that, by the law of the elder line, Darragh ruled by mistake. Gerallt did not know of Einion's pledge."

"Who deceived him?" Gwynedd said, rising from her chair.

Jeston narrowed his eyes at her. "I did not say that he was deceived. By the law of the elder line, long accepted in Acorra, the throne belongs to the heir of Einion. We have no law in this realm that requires men's words to be kept if they are not said in the presence of a witness or a scribe."

The tutor closed the book and looked out the window as Gwynedd lowered herself into the chair and folded her hands. After many moments of silence, she said, "Is our learning finished for this day, grandfather?"

Jeston turned and said, in a distant and slow voice, "You may go, Your Grace, if it is your wish. I have taught you little of our great realm, but we will continue tomorrow."

Gwynedd nodded, turned, and left the room after calling out a hasty farewell. Ciara, who was waiting by the door, gasped when Gwynedd rushed past her.

"I am sorry," the queen said.

"No matter," her servant replied. "How may I assist you, Your Grace? You appear distraught and anxious."

"Nay, it is not so bad as that," Gwynedd said, "but I do desire to speak with Eamon, the soldier who serves my uncle. He escorted me to this castle yesterday and there is a matter of some importance that we must discuss."

Ciara raised her eyebrows and opened her mouth, but after a moment she closed it and exhaled. "I cannot lead you to the barracks myself," she said, "but the door-guard, Captain Lochlann, might take you there. I will lead you to him."

Lochlann took her to Eamon, though he was wary of the new young soldier. "If you were not the daughter of my king, my lady," he said, "I would not allow you to speak with him unaccompanied. The people of the Glade-village have ever been tight-lipped and strange, and are often loyal only to their own folk."

"I will be guarded in my words, good sir, to ease your mind. If danger arises, I will endeavor to see that you are not thrust into peril."

Lochlann turned and furrowed his brow. "I shall not ask if your meaning is deeper than it appears, my lady," he said, "but I hope that you will keep your word."

"So do I," she said, but in a voice he did not hear.

Gwynedd stepped through the doorway of the barracks and, fortunately, saw Eamon at once. She kept near the wall so that all the men did not notice her and said, "Good sir, I must ask a favor of you."

The soldier nearly jumped in shock, and he let out a shout.

"Hush," Gwynedd said.

"I beg your pardon," Eamon said, bowing. "How may I be of service, Your Grace?"

"I wish to be led to my uncle and hear his council with the captains."

"Ah," Eamon said. "Then the rumors were true. I do not know exactly where the great Bindor has gone, but I will lead you to the place I have guessed."

They fetched their horses from the dark stable and set out to the south. A cold mist was beginning to fall, and it drove into their faces. Gwynedd wished she had worn a cloak. After some time, they came up to a hard ridge of gray rock and halted. "Listen," Eamon said. Gwynedd heard voices below.

"There is a clearing there where councils have often been held, or were long ago." Eamon said. "Only in times of war," he added, looking at Gwynedd grimly.

She looked down and felt sick. "We must get closer to hear what they are saying, but we will leave the horses here," she said, "so that we may hide among the rocks. The ridge will conceal us well enough, will it not?"

Eamon nodded. "Yes."

They swung out of their saddles and then hesitated. "There is nowhere to tie the animals," Gwynedd said.

Eamon looked in all directions and finally sighed. "We must walk slightly northwards and tie them to those gnarled trees. The stones there are tall enough to hide them." After they had done this, they went south once more and hid themselves.

Many men, leather-clad and powerful, stood around Bindor in the midst of the clearing. Gwynedd thought that her uncle, clad in a dark cloak with his hair blowing wildly, looked more like a wild pagan of long ago than an Acorran nobleman. But all thoughts fled her mind when he began to speak.

"Thus you can all see the gravity of our peril. No matter the number of Darragh's people, they have always been the fiercest of rebels, and they have begun in recent years to call the people of the Glade-village to their side. Great harm could come to our kindred if we do not act with haste. Arvel will slay our warriors in stealth and deceitfulness as his accursed father slew my brother!" His voice grew louder with every word, and he ended in a shout. The lords that stood around him let out a deafening, hoarse cry. "I must declare my brother's daughter Queen of Acorra before I can rally in earnest, but you may return to your provinces and begin to summon your people. By the time you have reached your lands, the crown shall rest upon her head."

Gwynedd shivered. Eamon, who was as gray as the mist enveloping him, looked at her silently. She looked eastwards, not wishing to answer him.

"We must go, my lady," Eamon said after a moment, "or he will find us."

She finally turned to him and nodded. "Yes. Let us make haste." They strode northwards as swiftly as they could without running and thus making themselves seen. Gwynedd snatched the reins off of the twisted branch so swiftly that the thin leather nearly tore, and though Eamon was less hasty, he too scratched the finely tooled bridle on the rough wood. They felt that it took them a hundred centuries to swing into their saddles, though it took no longer than before. If Bindor had been within an arm's length of them, they could not have been more anxious. After cantering for a few miles, they slowed.

"I hardly know why I was so frightened," Gwynedd said. She laughed, a flat sound without mirth that drifted off into the mist eerily.

Eamon shook his head. "Your Grace, fear should grip you like a vise. If you had not come to these lands, the lives of Arvel and his folk would not be at stake. And it seems to me that it is you who have endangered Bindor's kindred as well."

Gwynedd flung her head up. She trembled as well, but Eamon did not see it. He saw only her glinting eyes, not the shaking of her hands or the rough striking of her heart.

"Hold your tongue!" she said. "Their lives are not at stake. I will send a messenger bidding them to surrender, if they do not send one to me first, which they ought to do if they fear conflict. And I have in no way endangered my kindred. Only my own life is endangered."

"Your life, and the lives of all the men your uncle will force to defend it," Eamon said. He was pale, knowing the risk of his reckless words, but his jaw was clenched. "I would die gladly to defend a lady who had not brought peril upon herself by folly, but I do not wish to throw my life away because you are careless."

Gwynedd was white with fury. "How can you assume that this disaster came through my folly? I have done nothing wrong. If you intend to continue these foolhardy accusations, I will tell you the truth."

She sucked in a breath and then began speaking in a low, swift snarl. "I was wounded by an outlaw in the Silver Wood, and after struggling to journey on so that I could find safe lodging before nightfall, I was captured by the soldiers of Arvel. He refused to release me unless I told him my name and the name of my father, so I told him. He guessed that I was coming to join my uncle. Lord Bindor in turn assumes that the Wood-people will rise and attack now that they know Gerallt's heir is in control of Acorra; this is not necessarily true. The danger is not so great as it appears."

Eamon looked down. "Very well. I see not how you might have acted differently."

"And I am not finished, Sir Eamon. I have come to doubt your loyalty to my father, and this is a stain upon his honor. You must choose where your sympathies lie. If the Wood-people remain peaceful, you are right to refuse to attack them; but if they will not surrender, we have no choice but to strike."

Eamon nodded. "Yes, my lady. You are just." He remained silent until they reached the palace, however, and Gwynedd knew that he was not convinced. "I will tend to your animal," he said, taking the mare as the girl dismounted.

"Thank you," she said. He disappeared into the dark barn without speaking again. She rushed into the palace and slipped into her room. After attempting to dry her hair with a sheet, she put on a navy gown and soft leather shoes. Hoping the library was unoccupied, she made her way down the hall once more and through the room's broad doorway. The library was empty and silent. Gwynedd exhaled and went to a large bookshelf. She took a blue-covered, embellished volume and went to an oaken chair in a corner.

The Annals of Gerallt, King of Acorra, the title read. Gwynedd flipped hastily to the first page. *On this, the fifth day of the Ice-month in the nine hundred and twentieth Year of the Sundering, I, Gerallt son of Gethin, assume the Kingship of Acorra. My wife Enid will rule with me as Queen. Darragh, who was made king by an oversight by the scholars of Royal Lineage, will be informed of his displacement when he has returned from the island of Cormos. The Silver Wood will be his and his heir's as long as they remain peaceable toward myself and my kindred.*

After some time, he had written once more. *On this, Midsummer's day of the nine hundred and twentieth Year of the Sundering, I and my fair wife have been blessed, by the goodwill of God, with a daughter. She is called Gwynedd, and I name her my heir, even in the case that a son is given to me. On pain of their life, none must cross my will in this matter.*

Gwynedd flipped through the remainder of the book, but she did not see her father's flowing script again. After many blank pages, an entry began with a great blot. *On this, the twelfth day of the May-month in the nine hundred and twenty-second Year of the Sundering, I, Bindor son of Gethin, assume my duty as Chamberlain of Acorra until Gwynedd, daughter of Gerallt, is of age to assume the throne. The people of Darragh have forfeited their rights in the ownership of the Silver Wood because of an act of heinous violence against my kinsman, but action will not be taken against them until Acorra is united under my niece, Einion's heiress in direct line. Long may Acorra and its rulers endure, while the sun yet hangs in the sky!* Gwynedd leapt to her feet and slammed the book shut when she heard heavy footsteps on the stone floor.

"Lady Gwynedd, you are summoned!" a maiden's voice cried. After a moment of confusion, Gwynedd realized that it was Betrys. She darted between the bookshelves and met her servant in the doorway.

"I am here, and I will come," she said.

They tread the halls in silence until Gwynedd tapped the maid's shoulder. "Have you any idea why I have been summoned, Betrys?"

The servant shook her head. "Nay. I know only that it is a matter of great importance. Your uncle paces the floor of the great hall with his eyes flashing, and the servants have been sent to every corner of the palace on many errands. Or it was so when I was sent; I believe that all is quiet now, for they wait only upon you."

Gwynedd stopped short. "Should I not be dressed in a more fitting manner?"

Betrys turned and stared. "Of course you must, Your Grace. We are going even now to your chamber."

The queen exhaled. "Ah. Very well." They reached Gwynedd's room a few moments later. A gown of deep scarlet, gilded with the finest and most delicate patterns of flowers and trees, was laid on her bed. After Gwynedd put it on, Betrys spent a long time (or it seemed so to Gwynedd) weaving her hair into a heavy braid. At last, she was finished. Their footfalls seemed to echo thunderously in the silent halls, for the rest of the palace was silent.

The throne room was teeming with richly-clad lords and ladies. Gwynedd, despite her magnificent gown, felt small and insignificant. A sudden pang in her arm reminded her of Arvel, and she felt sick. "This is not right," she said.

Only Betrys heard. "Your Grace, what can you mean?"

But Gwynedd shook her head and trod the long path to the empty throne that Bindor was standing beside. He seemed grave, more grave than Gwynedd had ever seen anyone, but he smiled when his niece stopped beside him. Turning to a pale young man on the other side of the throne, he nodded. "The time has come." The man bent and lifted a golden diadem.

Bindor took it, then looked at Gwynedd. "For twenty years I have waited to stand by this throne and place the Crown of Einion upon your head, Gwynedd daughter of Gerallt. It has been worth everything." Gwynedd struggled to smile; her face felt like stone. She knew she could not speak and did not try. He set the crown on her dark hair and then motioned for her to turn. As she faced hundreds of keen eyes, she heard his voice ringing out triumphantly.

"People of Acorra, your hope has been fulfilled. The daughter of Gerallt stands before you as your queen, just as he wished. The road is yet long, and the battle is yet before us; will you pledge your loyalty unto her, and only unto her, while the sun yet hangs in the sky?"

The entire crowd seemed to jitter with pleasure. "To Gwynedd, heiress of Einion, Queen of Acorra, our lives are pledged! May we die before we break our vows!"

The queen was nauseous again, and every noise was far away like a sound in a dream. Everything in the room was hazy. The crown felt like an ice-cold chain against Gwynedd's forehead, and she knew too late that the golden trees of the Silver Wood had never caged her in.

She held her back straight until Bindor touched her shoulder and said, "The night is growing old, and we have no time to feast this evening. You may summon your servants and go to your chambers."

Gwynedd found that she could smile at last. "Thank you, my uncle." She descended the platform and slipped through the crowd as hastily as she could. Betrys and Ciara were waiting at the end of the aisle, and they led her back through the gray halls to her chamber. Gwynedd shivered. "Ciara, light a fire, if you please." The maid nodded and reached for the flint and tinder that laid beside the great fireplace.

Betrys said, "Beg your pardon, Your Grace; but shall I draw a bath?"

The queen shook her head. "Nay. I am weary tonight, and I wish to sleep. Fetch my nightgown." Betrys curtsied and obeyed. When the two girls left, Gwynedd sat up in bed and stared at the fire for a long time. Then her head became heavy and she turned over onto her side. The flowers etched on the wall seemed to sway as if they were blown in a strong wind, and it chased them into all of Gwynedd's strange dreams that night. She remembered none of them, however, when the gray light of dawn awakened her.

Three days passed quietly—nay, silently. Bindor's gray halls were uninhabited, save by the queen and a few servants. A downpour of cold rain fell relentlessly. Gwynedd spent most of her time in the library, where Jeston kept the fire roaring. She listened to her lessons, learned them without enthusiasm, and spent the remainder of the day reading. There were many prayer-books and hour-books, beautifully illustrated, that she pored over, and the books of maps and history were also wonderful.

Despite all this, she was uneasy at the end of the third day. She doubted that her uncle was away on a hunting trip for pleasure in the misty rain, and she was almost sure that he was rallying troops. That evening, he returned with his noblemen and called Gwynedd to a feast in the great hall. She went, for there seemed to be no way around it, but she ate little. Almost no one spoke, and the queen was glad to retire again to her chamber.

Gwynedd awoke the next morning when she heard shouting in the court-yard. It was so fierce that she leapt up trembling, threw a thick cloak over her nightgown, and rushed down the halls. She threw the great gates of the palace open and stood, gasping, in the doorway.

"What is this?" she said. A light-haired man in a blue cloak stood in front of Bindor and the pale young nobleman.

"A messenger of Arvel, the son of the murderer-king of the Wood-rats," her uncle said. His voice was a snarl.

"Uncle, I forbid you to harm him," the queen said.

She saw her uncle reaching for his sword-hilt. "You are in danger, Gwynedd. He is a liar and the messenger of a liar, and he has no good purpose in mind."

Gwynedd stepped forward. "Have you even allowed him to speak?"

Her uncle spat. "Do not be a fool; naturally I allowed him to speak. He has claimed that he is called Donan, and belongs to the court of Arvel, son of Darragh. His master sent him to propose a treaty: they will retain no Acorran land, except their principal village, in exchange for peace. Peace! How, you fool, can there be peace when you slaughter my brother, when you detain his daughter, when your accursed prince, the son of a murderer, will not relinquish his claim to the throne?"

Donan stepped towards Bindor quietly. "If we had known that the girl was the daughter of Gerallt and intended no harm, we would not have detained her. Neither Arvel nor his father before him cherished hatred towards your brother."

Bindor grimaced. "Only towards myself, I suppose?"

The messenger's eyes were burning. "Nay. Nay, though you stole all from Darragh, he cherished no bitterness. Though you put Arvel's very father to the sword by your bloodthirsty order, though he has spent years an orphan because of your malice and your refusal to believe Darragh, who was once like your brother, he cherishes no bitterness. None! He is yet willing to give all of his power to you in exchange for the lives of his people, for Acorrans, for your countrymen. But you would kill him." With every word, Donan's voice became more heated. By the time he had finished, he choked on his anger.

Chapter V

Donan's rage paled in the face of Bindor's fury. Gwynedd felt faint at the sight of her uncle. His face was like pale stone, and his eyes blazed when he turned to his niece. "Do you see? Do you not hear what he accuses us of? Do you not hear his scorn for your father? Will you still refuse to believe me?"

Donan looked at Gwynedd gravely. She looked away, but she set her jaw hard and said nothing to her uncle. Bindor reached for Donan's throat, but the young man jumped back. Then Bindor drew his sword with a guttural snarl and wounded the arm Donan held out to shield his chest.

The queen cried out and leapt forward. "No!"

Her uncle did not even turn to look at her before disappearing back into the palace, and the pale nobleman followed him. He had never spoken a word to restrain his superior. Gwynedd went to Donan, who was kneeling on the cold stone.

"I am sorry, my brother," she said.

His face hardened a little. "Nay, Your Grace-"

She straightened her shoulders. "Never call me that. Arvel is king. I will do everything—everything, Donan!— to give him the crown now. But you must go. My uncle will kill you."

Donan grimaced. "I do not doubt it," he said, "but my wound is no scratch."

Gwynedd sighed. "I know. I am sorry. Have you a knife?"

He pulled a short hunting knife from a leather scabbard, looking at her suspiciously. Gwynedd turned and cut a thick strip from her cloak and wrapped it around Donan's arm. "It will stop the bleeding, I think," she said. "I can do no better."

He struggled to his feet and nodded. "Thank you, my sister."

"God go with you," she said.

She knelt there, shivering, for only a moment before returning to the palace. Seeing Bindor in the entrance hall, she started. "I am sorry for my behavior, uncle," she said, curtsying deeply; it was difficult to keep her voice even, for her heart was on fire within her. After a moment, she glanced up and said, "This man Donan was courteous to me in the Silver Wood, but I forgot in my fright that such kindness is only his duty to me, and was poor repayment for detaining me in my own lands."

Her uncle nodded stiffly. "I am glad that you see this matter from my perspective now, Gwynedd. 'Tis perilous to parley with enemies so deceitful."

She lowered her eyes and curtsied again. "Yes, uncle. I crave pardon for my folly."

"I will pardon you. If the messenger had come in a more fitting manner and at a better hour, I would have consulted you and much pain could have been spared; but we must not regret it now. You may go to your tutor."

Gwynedd nodded and went to her chamber to dress before walking to the library. Her lessons grew shorter every day, and this reading lasted scarcely an hour. After Jeston agreed to let her go, she fetched her riding boots and her mare.

The horse was eager to be out of her stable, and Gwynedd rode northwards along the shore for some time. She thrust her hands into the mare's mane and dug her heels into her flanks when they came to a steep bank. As they crested the hill, she threw herself onto the ground and jerked on the reins to back her horse down the bank. Bindor stood on the sea-grass with the pale nobleman.

"Now that the rains have passed, my troops are eager," the young man said.

Bindor nodded. "Very well, General. You may take a small regiment to Darmor–taking the northern path that avoids Arvel's lands, of course– and rally them against the prince. I will rally a few more men and follow you soon after you have left; then we will attack him."

The general smiled, clasping Bindor's hand. "Thank you, sir. This day has been long in its coming."

"Indeed," Bindor said, "it has."

Gwynedd was sliding down the bank, dragging her balking mare along with her, as her uncle finished. After she had calmed the snorting animal, she vaulted onto its back and threw the reins on its neck. Its hooves made more noise on the sand than Gwynedd would have liked, but there was no help for it. She had to reach the barracks before the general returned to them; otherwise she would have to travel to the Silver Wood alone. Eamon, she knew, would come with her.

There were also men who had loved Gerallt but did not hold with Bindor, or so she believed. Jeston had endeavored to speak little of politics, but he could not conceal everything. It took Gwynedd many breathless minutes to reach the barracks, and she feared that the general was right behind her, but she unbolted the doors nonetheless. To her great relief, Eamon was there, speaking with a gray-haired captain near the doorway.

She went over to them as quietly as possible and looked at Eamon. "*Ekeron elteros bordontos?*" she said.

He raised his eyebrows– she was speaking in an ancient tongue only used by the people of Darragh, and had said only: "Is he loyal?" "*Dortonos holokos? Holany snaran untinli?*" he said.

Gwynedd furrowed her brow. She knew little of the Tongue of Siarl, but it seemed that he had said, "To whom? Are you attempting to trap me?" Hoping that her translation was correct, she said, "*Dortonos elte monarkikos, Artaravel. Lany necesco fortante tinli, Earmornon.*"

Eamon looked down. She had said, "To the king, Arvel. You must trust me, Eamon." Then he turned to his grizzled companion, who was gazing at the girl steadily.

"Yes," he said. "I was loyal to Gerallt, but I saw the messenger of Arvel fall with a deep sword-wound. I will not shed blood for your throne if you do not wish it, daughter of Gerallt. For I know that is who you are." His voice was low, but was in no way unsure.

Gwynedd started. "I am glad," she said, "and I will trust you, for I have no time to question you further. We must ride to the wood and tell the son of Darragh to ready his people for war. But for the sake of convenience, tell me your name."

The man nodded. "I am Torin, son of Tain; my father was a fisherman."

Gwynedd motioned for the men to follow her, nodding. "Very well. We must go with all haste; I fear that a young general, whom my uncle trusts greatly, will be here in moments. I saw him speaking with Bindor on the first North Cliff."

Torin furrowed his brow as he increased his pace. "And he did not come by the shore, I will guess, since *your* boots are sandy; you would not have risked such a perilous chase as that. Come along, boy," he said, turning to Eamon. "The way he took is shorter than the shoreline way. If you had not been on horseback, he would have outpaced you already; as it is, our time is short. Look out!"

Gwynedd's horse had untied its reins from the post by the side of the barracks, and now stood, snorting nervously, in the courtyard. The queen could see that her animal disliked the sound of her hooves on the hard stone. She caught the mare deftly, but her hands shook. Precious moments had been wasted.

Eamon and Torin fetched two rangy beasts from the dark stable, and then they led Gwynedd south to the thin path she had come to the castle by. There was no other way to take, but all three riders were uneasy. Often a stone that fell from the cliff to the left of the path resembled the sound of hoofbeats and made Gwynedd's heart freeze. When they came out into the sunlight, she exhaled and saw that Eamon was as pale as she felt. They both looked to Torin expectantly. He shook his head.

"I know not what path we should take. Which way was the general ordered to go?"

"North," Gwynedd said, "along the border of Arvel's lands."

The soldier nodded. "We will ride around the southern edges of the Glade-village and then go through the midst of the forest itself. Come; I fear that the rumbling I hear now is not the falling of stones." They galloped in single file, with the queen behind Torin and in front of Eamon. All seemed well until day began to wane and the horses became tired. The village was behind them, but there was a long strip of bare land that had to be crossed before they came to the edge of the forest.

"We could cross it now," Eamon said, halting his horse beside Gwynedd's, "but the animals are weary, and I do not like the thought of tarrying in the forest after dark."

The queen shook her head. "Neither do I, but we cannot remain here in the open. We will dismount the animals here and lead them. There are three of us, so we could alternate watches through the night, or–" she stopped.

"Go on, my lady," Torin said.

"We could press on until we reached Arvel's village," she said.

Eamon raised his eyebrows. "That would take us until dawn, if we were fortunate. We have ridden miles south of the village, and from the tales I have heard, it is a day's ride directly from the Glade."

Gwynedd sighed. "That is true, but I see no other way. We are not too weak to withstand the strain, are we, my grandfather?"

She smiled at Torin, who laughed. "Nay, we are not. Come, lad," he said, looking back at Eamon. "You do not fear the undertaking, do you?"

The boy laughed. "Nay, grandfather; but you may rue your recklessness sorely by morning."

The three wanderers reached the outskirts of the village an hour past dawn, stumbling and gray-faced. Eamon's exhaustion was relieved by leaning heavily against a tree, but Torin and Gwynedd threw themselves onto the damp grass and gasped for a few moments. The queen rose first. She pulled her disheveled hair away from her face, looking first at the village and then at Eamon.

"How many guards can you count?" she said.

He squinted and then turned to her grimly. "Fifteen at the least, my lady."

She exhaled. "I counted the same. They are on their guard. Far-roving soldiers must have met Donan, or at least heard of his injury."

Eamon furrowed his brow. "Donan? Who is this fellow you speak of?"

Gwynedd explained, and the soldier clenched his jaw. Torin finally rose as well, shaking his head. "All the more reason for haste, then, but I know not how we may enter the village alive. The prince is not likely to believe any tale you tell him, begging your pardon, my lady."

The girl looked down.

"Nay, do not beg my pardon. I know well that I do not deserve his trust, for I betrayed it recklessly."

Torin furrowed his brow, his pale eyes full of confusion. Gwynedd shook her head. "I will explain all to you later, grandfather. Now we must go on—after a short rest. There is only one course left to pursue. We must persuade the people of my village to join with Arvel of their own free will, without his rallying them. Only thus can he survive. They may not obey, but it is the only hope that I can see. Eamon, do you see any other way?"

The boy was quiet for a long time and then shook his head slowly. "Nay, though I do not like your scheme, it seems to be the only choice. Let us rest for an hour and then go on." The hour was short. If it had not been for the shade of the trees and the cool wind that blew east from the stream, Gwynedd could not have gone a step farther. Torin looked as if he had come to rue his recklessness as much as Eamon had predicted, and even the young soldier himself looked over-weary.

"Perhaps we should travel out of the sight of Arvel's village-people and then rest until afternoon," the queen suggested, struggling to her feet. "It is only a little distance to the Darmor-village once you can no longer see the settlements of the prince's folk. If we make haste, we may reach the outskirts of my people's town by nightfall."

Torin nodded and Eamon followed suit, though with less enthusiasm. "Very well," he said.

They found, to their delight, that the stream crossed their path after the village was behind them. It was enormously refreshing to feel cold water on their chapped lips and in their parched throats. After two or three hours, they were rested enough to go on—or Eamon and Torin were, and Gwynedd claimed to be. If their errand had been less urgent, she would have rested for twice as long, but her guilt burned within her. Every time her arm (which had not really healed) ached, the Wood-king rushed into her thoughts and she wished to gnash her teeth.

If I had only known, she thought as the night came on and they neared the forest's borders, *what would come of this! But I cannot be held responsible for my reckless uncle. And yet— and yet I knew in my heart that I was wrong. It was wrong to break my word, even if I did not know that I would endanger him. I knew in my heart that good would not come to him from my pride.*

"My lady," Eamon said.

"What?" she said. The harshness of her voice would have frightened any-one, and the soldier, whom she had spoken to kindly all day, flinched from shock.

"I beg your pardon," he said.

"Nay, I should beg your pardon," Gwynedd said. "I am sorry. What did you wish to ask of me?"

He nodded coolly. "I will forgive you. I wished only to tell you that we have nearly reached your village, and that it would be wise for us to halt and discuss our plans regarding what we shall say to your people."

Gwynedd nodded. "Yes; thank you, Eamon. I believe that it would be wise to say, 'The true king of Acorra is in danger of being attacked after he offered to surrender. I am the daughter of Gerallt, who thought he was the true king; many of you thought the same."

"I will not say that my father was mistaken, but I will say that I wish for King Arvel, son of Darragh, to keep his life and regain his throne. I beg of you all, rally and protect him! My uncle, a deceiver, intends to send his general to incite you against him. We must join Arvel's people before the general arrives, for then it will be too late. We will be surrounded on all sides, but it is our only hope. You must either murder your king or risk your life in the attempt to protect him. I beg of you to assist the Wood-king, for I will spill my own blood in the endeavor if I must."

She stopped short and realized that neither she nor her companions had stopped at the edge of the forest. They now stood in the middle of the town square, and a crowd of villagers stood before her. As she stared at them, she heard many quiet snickers and even more low whispers. But she kept her composure and looked them all in the eyes. "So how will you choose?" she said.

A sturdy, middle-aged fellow, whom Gwynedd had seen but did not know, stepped out of the crowd. "If the son of Darragh wished for us to join him, he would come to us himself," he said.

"Not if he was occupied in the act of rallying his own people and protecting those who are helpless," Gwynedd said. "And indeed, he is. I will ask him to come to you, although it may be too late by that time. If you will not join Arvel without his asking you himself, Bindor will come to you; and he may not give you a choice as I have done. You cannot stand only for yourselves. You must choose. If you will not believe my words, I will summon the prince." She crossed her arms and waited.

The man at the front of the crowd nodded. "Very well. We will lend you a horse."

"Excellent," she said. "I thank you."

Eamon came up behind her and grabbed her arm. "You cannot ride back into the forest tonight, and even if you were well-rested and had eaten, you could not reach his village in time to benefit anyone."

She lifted her chin. "I must try. I will eat if they will sell us anything, though I was not popular even before I claimed to be queen."

The soldier laughed. "I will attempt to procure something. Do not let them send you off before I have returned."

Gwynedd smiled. "No, I will not go off before you have returned, if you return quickly; but go now. The market is to the north, down that street. At this time of year, they sell until night has come on in earnest."

He went down the side street and disappeared into the shadows. The queen strode over to the nearest house and leaned against the wall. Though spring was even then becoming summer, a cold wind blew, and she shivered.

Soon the stragglers in the square became restless. The man Gwynedd had spoken to did return with a well-muscled black horse, but appeared to be the most ill at ease of everyone. After waiting a few moments, he looked at the sun and then came towards Gwynedd. "The day is growing old," he said.

She looked back at him squarely. "Yes."

He gazed at the red earth. "Perhaps it would be wise for you to set out, my lady, if you are determined to go."

"I beg your pardon, but I am hungry and weary after days of travel with no food. It will be difficult even after I have eaten; in my present state it would be impossible. I am not a strong woman at the best of times."

He glanced down at her slight frame and flushed. "I am sorry."

She shook her head. "Nay; I do not blame you. If I could—if I were even a little less hungry— I would set out at once."

Then she looked to the north. Eamon appeared from the dark street between the two houses nearest to her. He had a brown loaf in one hand and a leather flask in the other, but he looked ill-pleased. "This loaf of bread cost me—" he began hotly, then ceased, looking at the man holding the horse. "Here," he said, handing the loaf and flask to Gwynedd.

She ate as quickly as she could, followed the bread with swift gulps of water, and then took the horse from the villager. "I am ready," she said. Eamon held the stirrup while she swung into the saddle. She moved to nudge the horse's sides, but her friend caught hold of the reins at the bit. "What are you doing?" Gwynedd said.

"You cannot go alone, Gwynedd. And what an imp you have been, making me forget to think of it until now! I will ask for another horse."

Gwynedd shook her head. "We are straining our welcome. They were unwilling even to part with this one to such odd strangers as we are."

Eamon crossed his arms. "You dwelt here all your life."

"Yes," Gwynedd said, "but I am a stranger."

The soldier sighed. "I will come after you on foot and wait outside the town. If you are driven away, I will help you."

She shook her head. "No. I will outpace you by too much to make it worth your striving. It is too late, Eamon. I must go and meet the fate I have made for myself."

Chapter VI

Eamon helped Gwynedd into the saddle reluctantly. "I will leave Torin in the village and follow you at least for a little while, whatever you may say to dissuade me," he said.

"Very well," she said. "I am no queen, and I will not prevent you. But I cannot wait for you." She leaned forward and urged the horse on. It was a swift animal, and though Eamon bounded after her, she soon lost sight of him. After a few minutes in the forest, she wished vainly for a lantern. The shadows crept nearer and nearer to her, and the cold made Gwynedd shake.

"It is a cold spring for Acorra," she said, wishing fervently to hear the comforting sound of a voice. But when her words died away, she felt that the darkness had grown thicker and more menacing. *Those who seek comfort*, she thought, *will never find it.* She urged the horse to greater speed, and they wove through the trees in a rolling canter. Gwynedd knew it was reckless to go at such a pace, but hers was a small peril compared with that of Acorra and its king.

Gwynedd fell from the mare's back at dawn and crawled a little way to rap her pale knuckles against the palace gate. She was obliged to struggle to her feet and use the knocker, however, for her arms were trembling. As she leaned against the door and held her aching side, a guard flung the doors wide and she tripped into the courtyard. Then she straightened and wrapped her arms around herself. "I must see the king, Arvel."

The guard raised his eyebrows. "I have seen you before," he said.

"Yes, you have; but that is of no consequence now. If you will not take me to see him at once, take me to his sister Sinead."

He nodded slowly, scanning the folds of her cloak and dress. Then he raised his eyes to her face again. "I will take your word if you claim you carry no weapons."

She put her right hand over her heart, swallowing briefly. "On the honor of Acorra, I swear it. I would invoke greater names, but I am not worthy to speak them; and as for lesser names, my family's honor is worth nothing."

The guard nodded again. "I required no oath, but I see that you are earnest. Come with me."

She went out the gate behind him, and they went together until he bowed in farewell at Sinead's door. Gwynedd nodded in return and then went through the door. It was cold and dark in the great room, but Arvel's sister was in the corner kneading bread.

"I beg your pardon," Gwynedd said. "I have come to return the gown that you gave to me, but I will require another. I will pay this time." She held out two pale coins that Eamon had loaned her, wondering with a pang of fear if she would ever be able to pay him back.

Sinead looked at the coins and sighed. "I have no gown that is worth so little," she said.

"Nothing?" Gwynedd said. "Not even a thin shroud of rusty black?"

Sinead smiled. "Ah," she said, "you saw. When I gave you the green dress, you looked into the wardrobe."

"Yes," Gwynedd said. "May I go and fetch it and leave the green gown in its place?" Sinead nodded and took the coins, tucking them into a fold of her apron. Her guest disappeared for a few moments and returned shivering in the thin black gown.

She was holding her cloak closely around her, but she held her shoulders square and straight. "I thank you," she said, curtsying to Sinead as she reached for the doorknob.

Sinead followed her. "Where are you going?"

"I must see your brother, King Arvel," Gwynedd said, looking gravely at her friend.

She went pale. "I do not trust you, and I do not understand," she said, "but go. I see that your errand is urgent."

Gwynedd nodded as she shivered again. "Farewell," she said, stepping out the door. She wasted no time in getting to the palace, and she refused three guards' offers to show her to the throne room.

"I will reach it more swiftly myself," she said. Though the way was not very familiar to her, she came to the stone stairs in a few minutes and stepped down them quietly.

Arvel, who was standing at the window with his back towards her, turned at the sound of her footsteps. "What errand do you have in my halls?"

She looked him in the eyes. "I have come to warn you of the gravest peril. You see that I am dressed in black, my lord; it is not without reason. If some great miracle does not occur, I am the herald of your death."

His eyes widened as he came forward a few paces. He motioned to the door-guard, who brought Gwynedd a chair. Arvel lowered himself onto his oaken seat and leaned forward. "I wish for some sign to show that I may trust you," he said.

She straightened. "My lord, Bindor is marching out very soon with all the men loyal to him, intent on causing your destruction. If you do not set out at once and persuade the people of the village by Darmor to join your side, my uncle will rally them, command his men to attack from the west, and surround you. How, in giving you these tidings, could I wish to harm you?"

He shook his head. "If even the breath of a rumor was loosed that I intended to oppose Bindor, he would have an excuse to destroy me. This would be a very clever trap."

Gwynedd looked down. "My king, I know that the word and the honor of a usurper's daughter is of little value, but I give these to you. My father was slain—I will not say justly, for no man has a right to another's life— but not without reason. Yours was slain without reason. He was king by right, by the laws of honor and the weight of Einion's pledge."

Arvel nodded slowly. "I fear that you will make me trust you again," he said, setting his jaw. "You treated my trust poorly enough the last time I gave it to you, if my guesses are not mistaken."

"Yes, I did," she said, "wretch that I am. I allowed my uncle to proclaim me queen in the sight of all his people; if I had not done this, he would not have the power to rally all of those who were loyal to my father. But I am sorry." She got out of her chair and fell to her knees. "My king, I am sorry."

He put a hand over his face and sighed. "I have no hatred for you," he said, "but your sorrow will not save my people."

Gwynedd rose. "Perhaps not, but there is one thing that may. I have spoken with the people who live in the village by Darmor, and they said that they would follow you if you came to them yourself. Time grows short, however; you must choose if you will take me at my word."

Arvel rose and looked at her. "Yes," he said, "I will. I would say that, if you betray me, my trust will not be yours again, but if you are lying I will have no trust to give, nor will I have life. And now, since my life is already in your hands, I will place it there more securely. Go back to your uncle's lands and quiet his suspicions of where you have been in the best way you know how."

She nodded. "I am at your service, my lord." Then she went through the dark halls into the dim light of morning.

After fetching her mare, Gwynedd set her face to the west and set off at as quick a pace as the tired horse could muster. She journeyed for a day and a half, stopping only to finish her loaf of bread and drink at the streams that ran near her way. When she came to the castle by the sea, it was high noon, and the glare off of the water nearly blinded her. Faint and dizzy from exhaustion, she was terse with the guard that took her horse. No such peevishness could be used with Bindor, and when she came to the throne room where he sat, her terror had to show itself for what it was. She trembled and began to weep, which would have mortified her if not for the fact that it went well with her tale. "My lord," she said, "I have been following two deserters, who have fled far away. I lost their trail and was forced to return to seek help."

He raised his eyebrows. "Why did you not seek help before you set out?" he said.

"The soldiers in the barracks were all gone," she said.

"Where did the deserters flee to?"

She sighed. "Southeast. They seem to have ridden for the southern end of the Silver Wood; perhaps they wish to make for the sea and flee Acorra."

Bindor snapped his fingers at the guards standing near him. "Speak to the man who tended to her horse," he said.

They came back swiftly, though it seemed to Gwynedd that they were gone for hours. "The animal had a twig from the ceirian-tree caught in its tail, my lord," one of the guards said, "but the lady said that the deserters fled through the forest. It proves nothing."

Bindor rose from his throne, exhaling deeply. "On the contrary; it proves everything. It would have taken her far longer than this to reach the south-ernmost tip of the Silver Wood, for it does not extend as far westward in the south. She could not have gone much further south than Arvel's stronghold, though perhaps she went further east. Was there red mud on the hooves of her animal?"

The other guard, who had not yet spoken, nodded. "Yes, Your Grace."

Bindor looked down and made a low growl. "She rode to Darmor." Then he stepped forward and grabbed Gwynedd's shoulders.

"Tell me the truth," he said. "You journeyed with the two deserters to the village by Darmor and persuaded them not to join with my general in attacking Arvel. And then, perhaps, you told the scoundrel himself the danger he is in and begged him to oppose me, to oppose your side, to oppose your kinsmen?" He shook her. "Speak to me now!"

She set her jaw and spoke evenly. "No, my lord. I attempted to rally the villagers to King Arvel's side, but they would not follow me. Then I asked Arvel himself to rally them, which even now he has done, if he was not prevented."

Bindor, who was scarlet with anger, regained enough composure to turn to the guards and say, "Is the general still away? Has he sent no message?"

"No, sir," the guard said.

Bindor smiled; his gladness was horrible. "He has been prevented, then." He shoved Gwynedd. Though it was not a hard push, she was weak and tired, and she fell into a table with a crash. Bindor glanced at her briefly and nodded to the older guard. "Take her away, or she may escape again; but have a care and feed her something first."

The guard obeyed the first command, but he utterly disregarded the second. He led Gwynedd to a windowless room and slammed the heavy door without throwing her a word, much less a scrap of food. After a few hours of cold and silence, a different guard returned. Gwynedd thought he was rather sullen-looking, and he limped as he led her through the dark halls and out into the night. They went to the northwest corner of the palace, where he thrust open a small door. He motioned for her to enter it. There was nothing else to be done; she held her breath and stepped into the yawning darkness.

She brushed her hands against the damp walls. They were so smooth and cold that she thought they were ice for a moment, but the passage seemed to simply be hewn of sanded stone. Then she bent down and reached into the dark. She felt a wide ledge, and, after crawling onto it, she leaned down and felt another. Not wishing to miss a step and fall into blackness, she continued in this way until reaching the bottom.

"I do not know," she said to herself, "why I climbed all the way down here. It is damper and colder than the first step. But then again, I could not have been expected to sit cheerily on the edge of what I thought was a great abyss. Yes; I wished to find out if there was a floor. Here it is." She sat in the corner and slept for what seemed to be only a short moment. When she opened her eyes, a flash of light streamed through the passageway door and caught her attention. Stumbling to her feet, she parted her dry lips.

"Escape," she said. "I must escape." She began to crawl up the steps. They were rougher than she had realized, and she cut her palms three times in her haste. By the time she had reached the top step, she had to kneel for a moment and catch her breath. Then she gazed through the crack in the door. It was a disappointing sight. She had clung to an unlikely hope that Torin (she could not hope that Eamon would be spared from the battlefield) had returned to save her, and that the light she had seen was his lantern. But it was only a sliver of light streaming from the thin moon.

Her hands shook. She did not want Arvel and his soldiers to die for her pride while she waited in safety, even if she was eventually left to starve. Soon she began to feel like weeping, but she did not want to. To prevent it, she began to sing brokenly. It was a very old song, but she had only heard it once, on a long ago night in a silver forest.

There lived a king by the sea
And it roared and tossed, the foaming sea
And he ruled a land that was fair and free
But he comes no more to the sea, the sea
Oh, he comes no more to the sea.

Then she shivered. Far away a wolf had howled with a voice deep and cold. As she leaned against the door, she strained to hear the sound of the sea crying. Suddenly she stiffened. Footsteps, deliberate and heavy, were crunching on the sandy soil.

He shall come no more to the sea, the sea,

But the land again shall be fair and free
When a king dwells again by the sea.

Someone had finished her song in a husky, off-key voice, but it did not unnerve her. There was a comforting familiarity to it. She pressed her face to the door and let her eyes rove over the little space she could see. On the left side of her view, the blonde crown of a man's head appeared. His face could not be seen; he was bending over the lock and tinkering with it.

"Who are you?" Gwynedd said.

"Donan," he said. "Torin wished to come and assist you, but Eamon insisted that I should come. Torin may be of some use in the battle, and I would be of none."

"How did any of you know?" she said.

He looked up, stopping his work with the lock for a moment. "Know what?"

She lowered her eyes. "That he had imprisoned me. And why would anyone take the trouble to rescue me at such a time?"

Donan bent to work on the lock again. "Eamon and I crossed paths in the forest; he was following you, and I was attempting to join Arvel. We did not *know* anything, but we guessed much. And we agreed that it was only a guess. I met with Eamon in the forest, and he had met with Arvel; together we decided that you had no chance of remaining free. If Bindor is triumphant in battle and we leave you in his hands, he will continue to use you. On the other hand—"

The lock clicked, and he paused to smile. "On the other hand, if Arvel can be kept safe and Bindor does not have the leverage of your name in his grasp, your uncle's power will be greatly lessened, and the House of Siarl, if we are fortunate, may regain power."

Gwynedd was quiet as Donan swung the door open. After climbing out of the darkness and getting to her feet, she looked at the soldier. "Will he kill me?"

Her voice was soft, and Donan thought that he had not heard her correctly. "What did you say?"

"Will your king put me to death?" She looked down and bit her lip after her hasty question.

Donan put his hands on her shoulders. "No. No. He also crossed paths with Eamon, and he was the one who guessed your plight first and made the wisest part of the plan. I will take you to a fortress in the northwest, where his aunt Mailana and her husband live with their son. It is the safest place for one of Arvel's allies to dwell in all Acorra; perhaps the only safe place."

Donan looked at her for what seemed like a long time, and she felt constrained to lift her eyes. "That is more than I deserve."

The soldier shook his head. "After what you have done, my lady, the king cares greatly for your safety. If he cared half as much for his own, I would have real hope of his regaining the throne; but now I fear, despite my bold words, that I can only wish for Darragh's people to be treated kindly by the Heiress of Einion."

She shook her head. "If it comes to it, I will do everything in my power; but let us journey on now. If the son of Darragh survives this battle, you may hope for a brighter Acorra than I could ever give you. But it will be a hard-won hope," she said. Her voice had died away in a whisper.

Chapter VII

After an hour of hard riding on fresh horses, Gwynedd saw that Donan's wound had taxed him more than she had thought it would. She cut in front of him and forced him to pull his horse up.

"What are you doing?" he said.

"Tell me the truth, brother," she said. "Did your arm heal in the least before you left the forest and journeyed here?"

He looked down, growling a little as he clenched his jaw.

"Donan, look at your hand."

It was limp and gray. Donan exhaled. "Lady Gwynedd, what would you have had me do?"

She shook her head. "I would have asked nothing different from you, but now I must stop you. Dismount your horse and go to the Glade-village, or you will lose your arm. You have lost so much blood, I believe, that you could not go much farther if you tried."

He began to obey, but he stopped with one foot in the stirrups. "They will kill me."

"No. One of the men who accompanied me to Darmor was the son of the leader of all the Glade-people, and he was infinitely loyal. They are all, I think, more inclined to the people of Darragh than to the people of my father."

He swung to the ground, but paused again after catching his horse's reins at its bit. "Make the old man take you to Mailana. If you are anywhere near Bindor's troops, camp, or spies, they will imprison you before you can take a breath. He will give anyone half of Acorra if they turn you over to him. There is little, it seems, that he can do without saying it is your will and making his people believe that you truly ordered it."

She nodded.

"Oh, there is one more thing you must remember. If you see Arvel," he said, smiling for the first time since he had opened the dungeon, "tell him that one of his people, at least, would not mind bowing to a king *and* a queen."

Gwynedd swung around. "Pardon me, sir, but I will say no such thing!" she said.

Donan laughed. "Farewell, fair lady. May your path cross mine again before its end."

She nodded. "I hope that it will cross yours once more, but I fear that there is little of it left."

He shook his head, his eyes becoming very grave. "Perhaps; all paths must end. It matters little; yours will end in light. All will be well. Now I must go, and you must hasten. Be cautious."

He turned away and did not hear her say, "It is too late for caution."

Gwynedd knew that the north road was dangerous, but the south road was far too long for her to reach Arvel in time, and the straight path through the wood would likely be infested with spies. She turned her horse's head northwest and spurred it on. A storm began pursuing her from the east, darkening all the sky and crashing vehemently. Soon it was upon her. The little gelding that she sat astride began to stumble on the slippery path, and her flimsy dress was soon soaked through.

On her left, the silver trees were withered from the northern winds, and on her right stretched the gray, barren Plains of Drokond. As she continued on, it grew steadily colder; the path was rising higher. Gwynedd no longer wondered why the north road was said to be so dangerous. A sheer rock face of one hundred feet dropped off into a deep ravine as black as an abyss beside a path that two men could scarcely walk abreast on. Gwynedd was glad she had saddled a lean, narrow-chested horse. If he had fit onto the path with any less room to spare, Gwynedd was sure that they could not have reached their destination. The north road opened up into a wide gray field some miles north of Darmor. Gwynedd had meant to ride south after reaching the end of her path, but as she pulled the horse's head around, she heard hoofbeats behind her.

"After the girl!" a young man shouted. "It is Gerallt's daughter!"

She swung around and got a good look at her pursuers before urging her horse back into a gallop. Bindor's pale general was heading an army even larger than Gwynedd had expected, and they were pursuing her to Darmor. There was no chance that she could outpace them, but she hoped to join whatever troops Arvel had rallied and turn to fight her uncle's people before she was struck down. Sooner than she had expected, she came to the front of the Wood-king's army. Nonetheless, it was too late. Her journey had taken more than a day, and the sunlight was dying; as Bindor's and Arvel's armies clashed, she was unnoticed and caught between them.

"I must not," she said through gritted teeth, "die like this." She was still with her uncle's people. Glancing to her left, she saw an opening and spurred her horse towards it.

The animal's nose was past the ranks, and it was turning obediently towards the other army when a rider cut in front of Gwynedd.

She looked up into Bindor's face. "You are the daughter of my brother. I did everything to keep you on my side, but you have given me one choice: a choice between my brother and his child. There is only one way, Gwynedd."

All this was spoken swiftly. Gwynedd could have said a thousand things, but she was exhausted and paralyzed by the noise of battle on every side. All she could do was straighten and say through gritted teeth, "You cannot kill me."

Bindor shook his head. "You are mistaken. I—" Even in the low light, she saw emotion struggling within him. Anger and pain were rising in a hot flush on his cheeks. He blinked. "No. Not when my brother looks at me through your eyes. But I cannot let you help the murderer's son. I am sorry."

Gwynedd knew he would act rashly, but she was hemmed in on almost every side. When he pivoted his horse towards her and brandished his spear, she did not have time to break through the tiny gap on her right. For a long moment, Bindor's spear head was pointed at her chest. He was only two paces from her horse's head when he turned the end of the shaft towards her and shoved it into her side. She flew through the air and hit the cold ground. Surrounded by thundering hoofbeats, she knew that she would die if she did not escape the ranks. With trembling arms, she crawled over the frozen mud and dragged herself behind a stone. After a moment of painful gasping, she fell into an unconscious heap.

The battle went on to midnight and far past it. Arvel had utterly disregarded the begging of his people, riding at the very head of his troops. Eamon, too, struggled up to the front and fought there bravely; Torin could not manage such feats of heroism, but he held a difficult position at the east flank. They all fought on in the dark, confused and dizzied by the battle cries on all sides. Even the servants of Arvel's household had come to assist him, but Bindor had the advantage of numbers nonetheless. The Wood-folk listened many times to the heavy tramp of reinforcements marching in from the north. At daybreak, the armies called a truce; Arvel knew that he could not hold his ground much longer if his troops did not regroup.

As Bindor's soldiers passed their rations from hand to hand, a burly captain noticed the scarlet-stained ground in front of a great boulder. "Ah, some foolish boy from the Wood-king's ranks tried to desert and was wounded, no doubt," he said, nudging his companion and pointing to what he saw.

"Perhaps," the other fellow said. "We ought to see if it is otherwise, however. Perhaps a great captain was hurt in the night and, knowing he could not be helped until morning, was forced to hide. Such a fellow could be worth a ransom, it may be."

The captain nodded. "True, Oisin; let's look while we're able." They wove around their comrades, taking care not to be noticed, and soon came close enough to peek behind the stone. Oisin went a bit closer than the captain did.

"Take care!" the latter said. "He may be armed."

"Oh, leave off your cowardice," Oisin said. "He is wounded, and even if he were not, I too am armed. Armed well," he said with a smile, patting the hilt of his handsome weapon. He strode around the rock and stopped, shaking his head. "I do not know how she came to be here, but it is only some young girl who met her end among the ranks; struck by accident, I am sure. It is a shame, but there is nothing we can do."

Oisin turned to go back to the troops, but two other men had followed him and now stood beside the captain. "'Tis a slight girl, dressed in a dark garment, is it not?" one of them asked.

"Yes, Mael; what of it? If she was yours, a little wife who was trying to follow you to battle in her youthful courage, I offer my condolences."

Mael shook his head impatiently. "Nay, but I saw how she was killed–injured, I ought to say, for she did not die at once. Bindor struck her with his great spear and threw her from her horse."

"'Tis a foul deed, to be sure!" Oisin cried.

The other man with Mael shook his head grimly. "It is fouler than you guess. Did you ever see the face of Gerallt, Oisin?" Oisin nodded.

"To be sure, Naal; you ought to have known that."

Naal nodded towards the limp woman on the ground. "Look at the face of the girl, Oisin."

With his brow furrowed in perplexity, Oisin looked. Then he cried out and went gray. "It cannot be. 'Tis his very likeness– could it be–"

Naal sighed. "I fear that it is his daughter, his only heir, the Queen Gwynedd. I do not wish to speak ill of her uncle, but my heart forebodes that he did not strike her by accident; he meant to usurp her power. I, for one, will no longer answer to such a man."

"Nor I," Mael said.

Oisin shook his head. "Innis and I cannot either, for we were with Gerallt on all his campaigns and will submit to no one else of his family, now that the girl is dead. The Kingly Line of Einion was true to the ways of Calev, but those who were not in direct line to the throne have ever been strange and shifty. It is they who have always been cruelest to the House of Siarl, as we see even now. I am finished with needless bloodshed," he said, looking grimly at the girl.

Mael sighed. "Should we bury her?"

Just then the call of a horn sounded over the gray fields. Naal, who had been staring into the distance, turned to his companions. "We should return to the troops, lest we be put to death for deserting and prevented from helping Arvel." Innis and Oisin glanced at each other, their eyes doubtful, but they followed Mael and Naal loyally.

After the men were gone, Gwynedd sat up and leaned against the stone. Her head throbbed, and her side was badly bruised where her uncle had struck it. The blood that the men had seen had only been from a cut on her arm; she had hit a sharp rock when she was thrown from her horse. She ripped the hem from her dress and bound the wound, then shivered. The soldiers had begun to shout challenges from across the lines, and soon the *swish* of a sword being unsheathed was followed by the hard beating of hooves. Gwynedd knew that she could not leave her hiding place; if she fled west, she might be seen and captured, and all other paths were cut off. She lowered her head to her knees and covered it with her arms, leaning close to the boulder and hoping that wayward arrows would not strike her. However, after the sounds of battle had gone on, in all their raucous cruelty, for a few moments, all noise except the cries of Bindor's men went quiet.

Gwynedd leaned around the corner of the boulder and looked out over the battlefield. Arvel's men had ceased fighting, though they stood in tense readiness, their hands tight on their sword-hilts. Bindor, who had been galloping to the front of the ranks, had been stopped and was hedged in by fifty gleaming swords. More than half of his men stood before him, weapons drawn and eyes blazing.

"Why did you strike the daughter of Gerallt?" Mael cried.

"She was going to the side of Darragh's son," Bindor said.

"If our king's daughter wished to ally herself with Arvel, allowing him to keep his lands and safety, you should have let her lay her case before us."

Bindor tried to slap Mael across the face, but he jumped back. "I was," Bindor said, "to allow my niece to ally herself with the son of her father's murderer? She would not forgive his wrongdoing; she would ignore it or believe his lies. She would believe that Darragh did not do it, that it was Arvel who had been dealt a cruel fate. And why? Because the golden-haired boy has turned her head. She is a foolish girl, and I had to protect her life and her father's honor."

Mael stepped forward again. "What of it? There are some among your people who would not think her judgment wrong. You seem to have forgotten that Gerallt, too, trusted Darragh and his people, and loved his little son as his own."

Bindor snarled. "Of course he did. Gerallt trusted the mongrel, the traitor, the usurper right up to the moment that Darragh ordered his death. That is how your queen would have been treated, brazen Mael. The alliance would have been her suicide, and anything but Arvel's death will be suicide for Acorra."

Mael stopped his men from striking Bindor. "Restrain yourselves, and leave off acting like a pack of wolves. Take him from his horse and bind him; then we will let the king judge him."

Mael's men stepped forward, but the other half of Bindor's army gave wild war-cries and began to turn against their comrades. "Death to the traitors!" they cried. Some of them began to gallop back toward Arvel's troops, shouting, "Death to the mongrel, the murderer's son!"

Arvel's men were ready for them, however, and they now held the advantage of numbers. Struggling to break through the ranks, they succeeded, and Bindor's men began to scatter. It took a grueling two-hour battle to reach Bindor and his betrayers, nonetheless; their enemy was strong. When Arvel and his men came to the harried circle of insurrectionists, they were drenched with sweat and blood.

Mael, wounded but straight and proud, smiled at Arvel. "Judge your enemy, my king."

The king glowered at Bindor, who was bound and kneeling before him with a deep scowl furrowing his forehead. "You did not shirk from killing a woman so that you could ensure my death, Bindor son of Gethin; you have given your life into my hands, and I have every right to take it from you." His sword was still drawn; he had not sheathed it after battling through the ranks. Now, however, he slid the blade back into the scabbard.

Then he turned to his captains. "We will take him to my uncle's palace; he has many guards of great diligence. He will be imprisoned until he can be trusted, if such a day ever comes." Arvel paused and then went on in a lower voice, stepping towards Bindor and clutching the collar of his cloak. "Every day," he growled, "as you sit in that dungeon, think of the woman that you deprived of the right to do even that–you could not have bound her to sit in the darkness. You took her very life. Do not forget it."

Bindor's scowl deepened. "I did not kill her intentionally; indeed, you do not know that she is dead." Arvel turned away, the flush of anger slowly draining from his face and being replaced with pallor. He shook his head.

"Say no more, sir. I saw your brother's daughter fall." He turned to Eamon and his captains. "Take him and guard him until a party is readied to take him north."

Gwynedd saw the flash of disobedient hate in the soldiers' eyes, and she did not wish for her uncle to be slain because she was a coward. She came out from behind the boulder and ran swiftly across the field, then knelt before Arvel and the soldiers who had seized her uncle. Looking up only at the soldiers– she knew that the king would not harm Bindor–she said, "He did not kill me, though he could have. Do not slay him."

The men were speechless, but after a moment they nodded. "Yes, my lady," they mumbled as they took Bindor away. Gwynedd rose slowly, feeling that the eyes of Arvel and his army were on her. After a moment, she turned to the king. "I am sorry, my lord," she said, gesturing over the battlefield. His army had not been without losses.

He nodded, bowing slightly. "I will forgive you, my lady. If you had not come, our losses would have been far greater; perhaps our destruction would have been complete. As it is, I am almost in your debt."

She smiled sadly and shook her head. "You will never be in my debt, my lord."

He gestured to her arm. "You have injured your other arm. I am surprised it was not broken when your uncle struck you."

She looked down. "He struck my side; my arm was merely cut by a stone."

Arvel furrowed his brow. "Are you injured badly, my lady?"

She flushed. "I do not think so, my lord."

The king motioned to Eamon. "Let us find the lady a horse, lad." As he followed Eamon, he turned back to tell Gwynedd, "My sister will care for you in my village. If we set out now and take a short path, you may be in her home by nightfall." He lifted his hand in farewell before turning away, and Gwynedd nodded.

Soon Arvel and his men were ready, and they escorted Gwynedd, along with many of those who had betrayed Bindor, along the forest path. The girl rode beside Arvel at the head of the soldiers. "Almost all of those who betrayed my uncle are with us," she said.

"Yes," the king said. "Does this concern you?"

She looked down and shook her head. "I do not know. Is my uncle well-guarded?"

"Certainly. Fifty strong men are standing watch around his tent, and they will take him to be imprisoned in the north tomorrow morning."

"That is well," Gwynedd said.

"You are still unsure, my lady," Arvel said after a long pause. "What concerns you?"

She turned and looked him in the eyes. "You saw that it was not Bindor who first attacked you. His troops were led by a pale young general until my uncle arrived with reinforcements, were they not?"

Arvel nodded, his face becoming grave. "Yes," he said, "I saw the general well. We were locked in combat for some time after he felled one of my best captains."

"Was the general found among the slain and injured?"

"No, my lady."

"What became of the men who did not betray my uncle?"

Arvel exhaled. "Many were killed, but more than half remain. They retreated and disappeared in the chaos surrounding Bindor's capture."

"How many were slain in battle?" Gwynedd said.

"Perhaps one hundred fifty."

The girl sighed and shook her head. "Then at least one hundred escaped. Half of his men turned to your side, and I would guess that his army originally numbered five hundred. Perhaps I am wrong; do you think?"

The king looked down. "I believe that you are right. Do you think that they are dangerous?"

Gwynedd thought for a moment. "I know that they cannot take over Acorra, even if they were to rescue my uncle from his imprisonment. However, I fear–"

They had reached the outskirts of the village, and three men came up to them with their copper lanterns jangling. The golden light was warm and comforting, and when the villagers cried out, "It is the king; he has won!", the houses too were lit from within and their shutters thrown wide.

Gwynedd smiled at the sight of the linlon-flowers illuminated by the candles in the darkness. "Your land is beautiful," she said, her eyes shining shyly at Arvel.

"Yes," he said, "'tis a good kingdom, ours."

Chapter VIII

Gwynedd awoke the next morning when the dawn was still young and pale. After realizing that she was in an upper room in Sinead's home, she sat up to watch the morning star until her hostess began to stir. The house was silent, and there was no sound in the village below. As she looked out over the golden crowns of the trees, Gwynedd felt as if she were the only person alive. A cool breeze flew through the open window, and a bird called; at last the sun rose and the day had come.

Sinead flung Gwynedd's bedroom door open and came in with a yellow dress over her arm. "'Twill be a warm day," she said, "too warm for your black dress, though I know it is thin. I never wear this gown, so you may keep it."

Gwynedd rose slowly and nodded. "Thank you, Sinead. You are kind."

Sinead, who had been turning to leave, stopped and gave a small smile. "After what you have done for my brother and my people, this is no overgenerous payment. Perhaps you do not deserve much gratitude, for you have only made amends for wrongs you began, but you have risked much, and I feel inclined to be grateful."

When Sinead had gone, Gwynedd put on her gown, combed her snarled hair with her fingers, and padded down the stairs in her bare feet. Her hostess was not in the kitchen, but she had left a loaf of bread on the wide table. A wooden cup, filled with cold water, was set beside it, along with a handful of berries on a white cloth. *I took far longer to comb my hair than I thought*, Gwynedd thought ruefully. After she had eaten, however, she noted that the floor was unswept, and she was happy to tidy it with the straw broom she found in the corner. Her side began to hurt when she had finished, and she leaned against the window sill to rest.

Just then, Sinead came through the front door. She put her hands on her hips. "You are here to rest, Gwynedd, and I find you with a broom in your hands!"

Sinead's entrance had been quiet, and Gwynedd, who had been lost in thought, jumped. The broom clattered to the floor. "I am sorry," she said. She was pale with pain.

Sinead shook her head. "Sit down at the table."

Gwynedd lowered herself into a chair obediently, and her hostess sat down across from her. "I only wished to be useful in some way," Gwynedd said.

"Because you feel guilty," Sinead said, "and you think that my brother and I require you to earn our favor. Perhaps that is, at least in part, why you saved him and our people."

"No!" Gwynedd said. "I did not. I did not expect to keep my life, much less to gain anyone's favor; I did what had to be done."

"Very well," Sinead said, "but I hope you do not think that you must continue to help us in return for your life."

Gwynedd looked down. "No. I hope that I wish to help you out of gratitude for your kindness. I hope that it does not stem from my pride or a wish for your favor. But I am human, and I am sorry for the times when my motives are wrong; I am sure they are often wrong."

She rose and went to the window again.

"You will not rest, will you?" Sinead said.

Gwynedd turned and smiled. "I would rather not, no."

Her hostess laughed. "Will you, at the least, sit down if I let you go outside?"

Gwynedd glanced out the window. "Yes; I suppose so."

Sinead went into a closet and threw out a blanket. "Sit by the stream, where it is cool."

Gwynedd caught the blanket and reached reluctantly for the door latch.

It was not a great distance to the stream, but Gwynedd was surprised that Sinead had let her go so far; it was a long enough walk to make her side ache again. She threw herself onto the blanket in the damp grass and lay quietly for a moment. The sun filtered through the trees onto her face; it was not shady enough to fall asleep, and Gwynedd did not like to lay down when she was awake. She sighed and sat up, leaning against a tree and looking down at the stream. If it had been deeper, she would have dived into the water. It was hot even under the trees, and she was uncomfortable. She felt that what she had done would never be forgotten—that she would always be striving to cover up her past wrongdoing with endless attempts to be good. Sinead had been right—almost every word she had uttered was true.

Gwynedd hugged her knees to her chest and began to cry. "Two hundred, perhaps three hundred," she said, thinking of the men who had been killed. Perhaps Lochlann, whom she had sworn not to thrust into peril, lay dead at this moment, and young Bearach was left an orphan. She had not seen Torin after the battle; perhaps the last hours of his long life had been spent in agony as he repaid her wrongs. As for the others, she did not know them and had never seen them, but they had sisters and mothers who loved them; some of them had wives and children; maybe some had been young men beloved by girls no older than herself. She thought of Arvel and then straightened, flushing and covering her face with her hands.

"Fool," she cried through clenched teeth, "fool, fool! Pity those girls, but do not pity yourself. If he had died, it would have been your fault, but those girls had done nothing. And he is alive, and he does not love you, and you cannot love him." She looked down at her trembling hands, then grabbed a piece of bark and flung it into the stream. As she watched it float away, she sucked in a long breath and pulled her hair away from her face. She gazed at the bright sky through the tree branches.

"I am sorry," she said. "It is You I should pity; I caused your death too, and You were truly blameless. You have forgiven me, and I know it, but I cannot believe it today. All I ask is that I might believe it tomorrow."

The remainder of the day passed swiftly, but not swiftly enough. A sudden rain shower drove Gwynedd back inside, where she remained with no books and few tasks until evening. Then Sinead was strangely willing to accept her help in preparing the last meal of the day. When the meat and bread were ready, Sinead said, "The wooden plates are in the chest, over there. Set out three."

Gwynedd whirled around to stare at her. "Three?"

"Yes," Sinead said, bending over the stove to hide her smile, "three. My brother often joins me for the evening meal."

Gwynedd flushed. "Oh. Yes, Sinead."

Sinead had to lean very far indeed over her cooking pots when she heard Gwynedd drop the plates (not once, but twice) and nearly trip over the chest on her way to the table; she was almost inclined to laugh. When she turned around, her difficulties increased. After glancing hurriedly at the window, Gwynedd had almost fallen over the floor on her way to the door.

As Arvel entered the house, he said, "My goodness, Sinead; what has come over you? Leaning over the table as if you are having a spasm, then beaming at me as you always do!"

Sinead glanced at Gwynedd, who was leaning against the door uncomfortably. "Hush, brother," she said softly, "I was laughing at Gwynedd, but I must stop now; I think she is truly vexed. Your coming startled her."

Arvel flushed. "Sinead, you are telling me tales; that is not true."

Sinead smiled. "Yes, it is, and you are making me wish to laugh again."

The king looked at the girl in front of the door again, his brow furrowed in vexation. "I have tried to be kind to her; surely she is not afraid of me."

Sinead shook her head. "I do not know, Arvel; she feels very guilty for all that has happened." She looked tactfully at Gwynedd, who nodded.

She much preferred for Arvel to think her afraid of him than in love with him. Sinead had known this, and she smiled as Gwynedd came to the table. Her grateful guest smiled back before lowering herself into the chair Arvel pulled out for her.

The three of them ate in silence for a few moments before Sinead turned to her brother and said, "I am very glad that you helped me find what became of Huilon, Arvel. You know that I was anxious, especially after I urged him not to go; he is not well."

The king smiled. "Yes, but he is no worse after the battle, Sinead. He said that his crops this season are growing beautifully, and that he will be a richer man than ever before by Midsummer." Arvel chewed his thick slice of bread with gleaming eyes, and Gwynedd saw Sinead smile as she lowered her gaze.

"That is why I had left the house so early, Gwynedd," Sinead said after a moment, "and I am sorry. I am sure that it must have confused you."

"Think nothing of it," Gwynedd said quietly, "for you should not have done otherwise."

There was silence around the long table for a few minutes. Then Arvel turned to Gwynedd and said, "I did not intend to tell you, my lady, until you were better recovered, but the men guarding Bindor were pursued by the general and his men."

"No," Gwynedd said, leaning her head against her hand and shutting her eyes. "Please. No, my lord."

"They defeated them; two of my men were injured badly, but they were on their guard and Bindor's general thought to catch them sleeping, so he was disappointed. Nonetheless, you were right. What did you wish to warn me of concerning them?"

Gwynedd swallowed quickly, becoming a little paler. "I fear that they may try to kill you. It is only a guess, and perhaps it is groundless, but I know how my uncle and his people have acted in the past." As she finished, her voice became low and bitter. She looked down at the table and clenched her jaw.

Arvel nodded. "Ah," he said, "if that is all, I am not afraid."

Gwynedd looked up, her eyes widening. "Arv–my lord, you cannot be so indifferent to your life. It is not right."

He smiled and looked at her gravely. "I do not consider my life to be of no worth, Gwynedd. However, I think that the good of my people is worth my life, if that is the price I must pay for it. I will not be reckless, but I have hidden in this forest long enough. I am a man, and I must do the work of a man; I should have done it long ago."

Gwynedd nodded at him timidly. "Yes, my lord. One cannot live in the fear of dying. I only wished to make certain that you would not be reckless."

The room was silent for a moment. Arvel finished his slice of bread and then said, "I am sure that you wish this for the sake of Acorra, my lady; but if harm comes to me, the crown could return to the Heiress of Einion. I believe that my people would be safe under your rule."

She looked at him incredulously. "My lord–"

Sinead cut in. "Arvel," she said, "your father was killed by Einion's people."

He gazed at her, his eyes a little hard. "Not by the heir of Einion, Sinead, and not by Lady Gwynedd. What if I was held responsible for the wrongdoings of my fathers? What if you distrusted me because of King Grathon's greed or King Padric's selfish cruelties? Gwynedd acted wrongly once in a moment of pride, and that is the only thing you may justly hold against her. She would be as worthy a queen as I would be a king. Of course, I will give you the throne if you wish for it, but I never knew you wanted it. What has come over you?"

Sinead was quiet for a moment. Then she said, "I am sorry. In my worry for Huilon, I became bitter towards Gwynedd, but I was wrong. I can give no other reason, but I—I have always expected you to marry and have an heir like other kings."

Arvel was silent. Sinead looked at Gwynedd, who was deathly pale, too late to prevent her mortification.

The king pushed his empty plate toward the middle of the table and rose. "I have never wished to," he said quietly. "The night is growing old, Sinead; I must go." Bowing to Gwynedd, he said, "Goodnight, my lady."

When Arvel was gone, Gwynedd's chair screeched across the floor. She turned to rush up the stairs, but Sinead was behind her and grabbed her shoulder. Gwynedd whirled on Sinead, tears streaming down her face. "What do you want from me? I know I am not worthy to be queen, but must you remind me of my wickedness and every wrongdoing of my family? I already live every day in shame. And then you must make it painfully clear that I am unworthy of your brother, humiliating me as I sit right beside him. Why?"

Sinead began to cry as she spoke. "I am so sorry. I did not mean any of what you said. You would be a worthy queen; I am sorry. I have been so afraid. And as for the other thing, I did not mean what you think. My brother—I—I did not mean what you think."

Gwynedd looked down. She nodded quietly, though there were still tears on her eyelashes. Then she laid her hand on the stair railing and turned to leave again.

Sinead's hand fell limply to her side. "I am sorry, Gwynedd," she said. "I am sorry that I humiliated you. Arvel loves you."

Gwynedd was halfway up the stairs, but she paused for a moment to laugh. "Ah, Sinead," she said, "you have made me smile at last. Do not worry; I will forgive you without being told tales. Goodnight; I am not angry with you. I am sorry that you were afraid."

Gwynedd was glad to go to sleep that night. Even the sharp aching of her side could not keep her awake. She woke, however, with the moon shining brightly in her eyes. She shivered. There were voices in the street below her window. For a few moments they all rose at once, loud and chaotic, but a clear shout silenced them.

Then whoever had shouted began to speak. "It is true. Fifteen men heard the general's plans from his own lips, for he and his men were near Mailana's walls. Twenty-five palace guards saw them set out towards the eastern mountains. If we do not set out and stop them before they return to my aunt's castle, there is no hope. We could not hold them off from inside the fortress; they would have numbers enough to hold us under a long and fatal siege. We must set out tonight."

Gwynedd would have known the voice even if Arvel had made no mention of his aunt. She rose swiftly, put on the black dress that lay on a chair, and went to the window. She had to lean a long way out to see the crowd in the street, but she was nonetheless surprised when Arvel stopped and looked at her. Catching hold of the window frame, she lifted her other hand in a quiet greeting. He nodded, a small motion that she could hardly see in the light of his lantern.

Gwynedd stole down the staircase and hurried to the palace stables. In her long, thick cloak, no one could see her skirts, and she knew that she would be unnoticed among the soldiers if she kept away from lanterns. She saddled her mare swiftly and snatched her bow and arrows from their place near her saddlebags before going out into the darkness.

Chapter IX

Gwynedd rode with Arvel and his soldiers all night. She could tell little about the lands they were passing through in the inky darkness, but from what she could determine, they were crossing wide fields with few trees and high, bare hills or mounds. When morning came, the men were still awake and ready to go on, but the horses were too weary to go any further without resting. The soldiers unsaddled the animals and tethered them to graze for an hour or two while they ate. Gwynedd had not had time to fetch any food before fleeing Sinead's house the night before, and even if she had, she was too weary to eat. Taking a long rope from her saddlebag, she slipped her mare's halter over her bridle and tethered it to a tree. Then she pulled her hood over her face and went to sleep on the side of the tree that was farthest from the soldiers.

She was startled awake an hour later by the sound of soft boots padding over the leaves. "We are riding on now," a voice said.

Recognizing it, she leapt to her feet. She flushed and looked down as she stepped around the tree trunk.

"I did not want you to be left behind, Gwynedd," Arvel said, smiling wryly. "If you did not want me to discover you, it might have been wiser to borrow another horse."

Gwynedd looked up, smiling a little in return. "I knew that you would recognize my mare. I only came secretly because I feared that your men would send me back."

He nodded. "Ah. And you knew that I would not?"

She nodded uncertainly. "I hoped you would realize that I am repaying only a small portion of my great debt to you."

Arvel stepped forward, his brow furrowed gravely. "My lady, you are not indebted to me. We are all indebted to our Lord, but there is no use in trying to repay Him. When I have done so little in comparison with that, why would you try to repay me?"

"I suppose," Gwynedd said, crossing her arms, "but that is quite different."

The king nodded. "Yes, it is different," he said, "but even if you will be determined to repay me, do not be ashamed of yourself. I forgive you. Your position was immensely difficult. I have often pitied your family and been unhappy that I must rob you of the throne that would otherwise have been yours."

Gwynedd furrowed her brow and leaned against the gray tree trunk. "You must not be unhappy, Arvel," she said. "I no longer want the throne. I hardly wanted it before, but—"

She looked away suddenly, squinting over the fields. "Your men are ready to ride on, my lord," she said quietly.

"Yes," Arvel said, nodding as he untied her mare and handed her the rope. He motioned for her to follow him, and she did so reluctantly. "Why did you wish to be queen, Gwynedd?" he said.

She flushed again as she looked down at the long grasses swishing against her skirt. "I had nothing else to wish for, my lord," said, "nor to hope for." She glanced at him gravely. "I am sorry, my lord. I know that I ought to have been more satisfied with my circumstances, more wise and grateful for all that I have, but I was–I was—" She bit her lip.

"What?" he said. They had nearly reached the soldiers, and she was able to avoid answering. Eamon handed Arvel his horse, neatly saddled, and he leapt into the saddle lightly. "Thank you, Eamon," he said. He watched Gwynedd pull herself onto her mare beside him. "Your arm still hurts you," he said, shaking his head.

She glanced at him, frowning. "Only a little."

He nodded. His men were gathering behind him in their orderly fashion, but Gwynedd's mare was too swift for her to fall back and join them. "You were telling me why you wished to be queen," Arvel said.

"Yes," Gwynedd said. "I was a shut-in, lonely child who became a shut-in, lonely girl. When my aunt died and Bindor's messenger came to me, a voice in me cried that I could be glad and beloved if I were queen. There was a quieter voice that thought otherwise; I knew it was the true one, but I did not heed it. My stubbornness has been paid for, but your people have borne the brunt of my debt. It is strange, is it not, how the selfishness of one maiden can kill half the soldiers of a noble king? Strange and unhappy; but such is the world."

Her voice died away in a low and bitter murmur, but the wind blew her quiet words to Arvel's ears. "You have forgotten that you did not wish for harm to befall anyone," he said. "And you have disregarded me. You are still ashamed. Every hour you seem to become more so."

She looked at him. "Perhaps I am, and perhaps I do. If so, I am sorry, my lord. But I am trying."

He smiled at her. "No; I am sorry. I will stop tormenting you, Gwynedd. We will speak of something else. Did you hear all that I said to my men in the square?"

Gwynedd nodded. "Yes, I did. I fear we are truly hopeless. If the general is able to rally even half of the men from the mountains in the north, he will outnumber you greatly."

Arvel looked down, nodding slowly. "Yes; there is certainly no hope of it being an easy battle. But it is not hopeless. If either you or I can survive and we can take the general, your uncle's people will scatter, and Acorra may return to the hands of a monarch who loves peace." He turned towards her, his eyes becoming graver. "Gwynedd, you saved both myself and my people. If only one of us is to return and rule this land, I wish for it to be you. If you must fight with us, stay in the midst of the troops. We cannot both risk our lives."

"No, Arvel!" Gwynedd said. "You cannot. I cannot let you die. I—"

Arvel's jaw tightened anxiously. "Go on," he said.

"Very well," Gwynedd said, almost inaudibly, flushing more with every word. "You know already; I have seen it in your eyes. I love you."

She looked at him. He smiled, and she felt as if time had stopped. Nothing existed but Arvel and the radiant joy in his face. After a moment, Gwynedd's anxiety brought her back to the world. The smile she had not known was there died away from her lips.

Arvel's face became grave again. "I know. I love you. You do not know what I felt when I thought Bindor had killed you. If the choice had been in my hands, I would have struck him down at that moment, but it was not. However, enough. What would you have me do now? I cannot leave others to stop the general, and I doubt that you wish to. I will lead the troops and you will remain in their midst. I am sorry."

"It may not be as grave as you think," a voice said from behind them. They whirled around in confusion. It was Donan.

"You should not be here!" Gwynedd said.

"What do you mean?" Donan replied. "That no matter how fast I rode through the wood, I could not have reached you so quickly, that my arm will be no use in fighting, or that I should not intrude on your privacy?"

"We mean all but the last one," Arvel laughed.

"Yes," Gwynedd said, "that we do not mind. But the first two are certainly true."

"No," Donan said, "once the bleeding stopped, my arm healed swiftly. It is not all that it was, but it will do. And I borrowed the swiftest horse in the

Glade to return to the forest; though I knew I would be too late to help in the battle, I did not wish to wait for news of it. When I returned, you were both gone, and as no one knew quite where you were making for, I came as quickly as I could to follow you."

"Very well," Arvel said. "I suppose you have heard the news by now."

"Yes," Donan said. "All of it. I cannot agree with the conclusions you have drawn, however. The men of the northern mountains are wild and have no training in battle. They cannot overcome your army."

"However ill-trained they are," Arvel said, "they are fierce and numerous nonetheless."

"We shall see," Donan said.

They did not make camp until late that night. Arvel told Gwynedd that they would only ride twenty more miles north, but he wished for the men and horses to be well-rested. Gwynedd nodded distantly, glancing at the troops.

Arvel looked at her keenly. "What troubles you?" he said.

She turned. "I have not seen Eamon since early this morning, and I know that he was with your men. I know that none of Bindor's people can have harmed him, but I still fear some mischief."

"Of what sort?" Arvel said.

"If I knew," Gwynedd said, smiling wryly, "my mind would be easier."

Everyone woke before dawn. Even the weariest—men who had been injured in the battle with Bindor—were too tense and restless to sleep until the sun broke over the sloping horizon. The army set out quickly over the hills, cloaked and silent. There was no sound anywhere but the swish of the long grasses as the horses jogged over the rolling land.

At last they came to the edge of a bluff, and Arvel looked out over a wide field. Gwynedd heard the high and lonely trill of a single bird as she stood in her stirrups and saw the king sitting tall and motionless in his saddle. He scanned the lands from east to west, and she followed his gaze. A great army stood on the edge of the horizon, high above the flat lands, in the northeast. It was silhouetted like a shadow against the fiery dawn. Gwynedd's heart froze.

A tall gray fortress could be dimly seen in the northwest. As Arvel looked at it gravely, Gwynedd guessed that it was Mailana's castle. If they did not stop the general and his men from crossing the plain, they would besiege the fortress. There did not seem to be any way, however, to reach the flat lands from the bluff. It stretched many miles to the east and west. As Gwynedd looked frantically around, Arvel turned his horse's head east and motioned for the army to follow. There was a path down the bluff– it was steep, zigzagging, and treacherous, but it was a path nonetheless.

Soon they were out on the plain, entirely exposed. Arvel shouted orders to his troops, and they got into formation. Gwynedd hardly heard him–her ears were ringing, and her pounding heart was choking her–but she positioned herself neatly among the ranks. She had no armor but a leather breastplate. Arvel had fetched his boyhood one for her on the night they set out; he had recognized her horse even in the moonlight. Though she was glad to have it, she wished for more protection. The general was leading his men over the plain. They descended in a clamoring horde from the northern ridge. The shouts of the men and the thundering of the horses' hooves combined in a deafening roar. Gwynedd heard the swish of swords being unsheathed all around, and she strung her bow.

Arvel raised his great sword high in the air. It gleamed in the light of dawn as if it were on fire. The king cried, *"Paran Ostonon Monarkikos!"* It had been Calev's rallying call against the pagans who besieged him in the night almost a thousand years before. It was what Siarl had cried when he galloped across the southern plains to capture a magician who had deceived his people. Darragh's father had shouted it when his traitorous courtiers had tried to kill his son. Now Arvel–the last king of the House of Siarl, and perhaps of Acorra, as he thought– said it again as his huge horse bounded over the grass, bearing him ever closer to his enemies. It was not a cry for Acorra, nor for that land's king. "For the Great King," it was often translated.

"*Diron Einion!* For the glory of Einion!" the pale general cried, thundering down the hill. His ranks crashed into Arvel's a moment later. The armies began to struggle. Gwynedd let five arrows fly before two hours had passed; though she was in the midst of the ranks, the general's men tried to break through the troops several times. The sun rose in the sky, and Gwynedd smelled the horses' sweat as the day grew hotter. Her own hair clung to her forehead, and her dress stuck to her damp skin under her breastplate. She strung her bow again, but for the first time, she was too late to stop the soldier from breaking through the ranks. One of Arvel's men, three soldiers away from her, fell and did not rise again. His horse bolted and scattered more men, worsening the gap in the troops.

The general's men began to inundate Arvel's troops. Gwynedd strung her bow and let three arrows fly in quick succession, but a horrible pit was in her stomach. She had only twelve arrows, and had neither a sword nor a knife. She would be utterly helpless when the enemy came truly close, and she could only hold them off until her arrows ran out. As she strung her bow and let another arrow fly, a movement to her right caught her eye. She choked. Arvel had fallen. He did not rise from the grass where he lay. She tore her eyes away and strung her bow again, but Arvel's men were on the brink of retreating. Many soldiers had been injured, and their horses had fled.

Gwynedd had used her last ten arrows. Only a hundred men (if that) stood around her, and half of them were injured. Arvel still lay motionless on the ground. The general began to fight through the ranks, and Gwynedd knew that he would come to her in a moment. She turned to the man behind her. "He only wishes to strike me. May I have your sword?" He nodded. "Yes. Take it." He laid it in her hands. She brandished it and watched the general.

He struck down two more men and was soon within twenty feet of her. Suddenly a movement on the horizon diverted her attention. The sharp call of a horn broke through the stifling air. After half a moment, two hundred men came thundering down from the north. Their horses were exceedingly swift, and the general turned when he heard the hoofbeats. He was struck down before he could move. His men began to scatter, and none tried to capture Gwynedd. Soon they had all disappeared into the northeast, leaving their injured and slain on the battlefield.

Gwynedd dismounted her mare, leaving the reins trailing on the ground and throwing her borrowed sword into the grass. She ran over the slippery ground and knelt by the fallen king. Donan and Eamon, who had led the two hundred men from loyal villages in the north, came and knelt beside her. Sick with dread, Gwynedd reached out a trembling hand to feel Arvel's neck for a pulse. It pounded faintly but steadily against her cold fingers. She choked, but regained self-control quickly and looked at Donan. "It is his shoulder that was pierced, not his heart, but he has bled a great deal. One of us ought to go to Mailana and ask for help for him and the other injured. I do not know about the others, but we cannot move Arvel. He will die."

Chapter X

Dark storm clouds had been gathering, and they began to thicken as Eamon fetched Gwynedd's mare (the least weary creature on the battlefield, for she had not galloped a stride that day) and set off for Mailana's castle. Donan and Gwynedd knelt by Arvel in utter silence. Gwynedd kept her hand on the king's neck, afraid that his pulse would stop at any moment. It did not, but it did not grow stronger either. Donan tore off the bottom of his cloak and pressed it hard against Arvel's shoulder. A steady rain began to fall, and thunder crashed behind the hills. The sky was almost black. Gwynedd was shivering hard, but she threw her cloak over Arvel.

Suddenly he awoke. His eyes were strangely bright, as if he had a high fever. He lifted his uninjured arm and touched Gwynedd's face, then saw that she had given him her cloak. "You must not," he said, "you are cold, my Gwynedd." He soon lost consciousness again.

Gwynedd shook her head and looked at Donan. "He will not live," she said. Tears began to run down her cheeks. She lowered her forehead to Arvel's chest and knelt without moving. Donan looked up at the dark sky and shook his head.

Half an hour later, Gwynedd looked up to see a golden-haired woman and a tall man leading a small party of people who appeared to be servants. Realizing she had not checked Arvel's pulse for some time, she reached frantically for his neck. "The same," she said, exhaling as she looked at Donan. He nodded, then looked west. Gwynedd followed his gaze and started with surprise—the party was upon them. She rose quickly and went up to the golden-haired woman.

"You are Mailana?" she said.

The woman nodded. "Yes, I am." To Gwynedd's surprise, she immediately dismounted her horse and went to her nephew. Gwynedd looked down quickly. She was reminded of a king who had descended from his throne to bind the wound of a trespassing enemy.

Shaking her head, she looked at Mailana. "Will he live?" she said.

The woman looked at her nephew's face. It had gone from feverish red to a pale gray. "There is no way of knowing now, but we will know soon. He will become either better or worse in less than an hour. Ingred, bring me my satchel, and come with your sisters and aunt to help me."

She looked at Gwynedd while she waited for her servants. "I have devoted many years to the study of medicine and botany, and my servants are wise and skilled. We will try our best." She gazed down at Arvel again. One of her servants knelt beside her, and the other two went to the king's other side. Donan rose to get out of their way and came to stand beside Gwynedd.

Mailana looked at the king's wound once and then glanced sharply at Gwynedd. "The blade that wounded him was poisoned. If we cannot find out what the poison was, I can do nothing."

Gwynedd went white. "Nothing–nothing–nothing–" seemed to echo throughout the valley, punctuated by a far-away crash of thunder. She sucked in a breath and turned to Donan.

"The general," she said. Before he could answer, she ran across the field to the place where the general had fallen. His sword lay unsheathed on the wet grass. Gwynedd, snatching it quickly by the hilt, took it to Mailana. "This is the sword of the man who struck him, I think," she said.

Mailana nodded slowly, taking the sword in both hands and looking over it. Then she turned to her servant and said, "Ingred, give me the flask of wine from my satchel and the two small, empty glass flasks."

"Yes, ma'am," Ingred said, handing Mailana the flasks quickly.

Mailana poured the wine over the sword and caught the runoff in one flask. After corking it, she laid it on the grass and filled the other flask with wine. Then she put a few drops of Arvel's blood into it. Both flasks soon became a dark green. "Wikanikon," Mailana said, looking at Gwynedd gravely. "If we cannot wash it all out of his wound, he will die." There were tears in her eyes, tears of real sorrow and deep pity. They ran down her cheeks in wide rivulets, and she had to wipe them away several times before she could see to begin treating the wound.

Gwynedd knelt beside her. "How may I help you?" she said softly.

Mailana stopped and looked at her. "You love him, do you not? You are his wife?"

Gwynedd went scarlet. "Yes, I do, but I am not. We have known each other only a short time."

Mailana sighed. "I wish that you were not here to see. I do not want you to— but there is nothing to be done about it now. You can hand me the blue flask and the long-leafed herbs in my satchel. They are my last hope for cleaning the poison away."After Gwynedd handed her the herbs, Mailana laid them on Arvel's wound and poured the blue flask over them. "Ingred," she said, "hand me the white cloth." Ingred did. Mailana held it against her nephew's shoulder and closed her eyes. "Ingred, go to the other injured men, and take your sisters and aunt."

The servant nodded, and she and her family left, leaving Gwynedd and Mailana alone by Arvel. Donan stood a little way off. Gwynedd looked at Arvel's face and closed her eyes. Then she sensed that Mailana had moved.

Her eyelids flew open. Arvel's aunt had pulled the herbs away and was holding a thick cloth to the wound. "Well?" Gwynedd said.

Mailana looked up. "The bleeding has stopped. If he regains consciousness in a few minutes, he will live. If he does not—" she shook her head and looked out over the hills. The storm had ended, and the sun was setting behind the ridge. The light it gave was pale—cheerless, Gwynedd thought—an unearthly light. She shivered. Suddenly she looked down. Arvel's eyes had opened. "Is it morning, Gwynedd?" he said, turning to gaze into her eyes.

She smiled, tears running down her cheeks. "Yes," she said, laughing. "It is morning."

The party returned to Mailana's castle with all the injured. It was dusk when they entered the courtyard. A young servant came out from a corridor and took Gwynedd into a high tower room. Its only window looked out over dark peaks in the east. When she had put on the nightgown the servant brought her, she leaned against the windowsill and gazed out over the land. Then she turned and went to bed, but not to sleep.

A grave week passed. The rain pelted down endlessly. Mailana did not need help, and the king still lost consciousness often, so Gwynedd paced the halls of the castle alone. They were dark, though the stones that paved them were beautiful and their walls were covered with tapestries. Not until the first day of a second week did a silvery light illuminate their high windows.

When a third week came, the sun returned, and the castle was bathed in golden light. Gwynedd found a passageway that led up to the high castle wall, and she went up to it. The guards smiled and made room for her to lean over the stone battlement. She looked out over the sparkling fields and sighed, a little smile on her lips. The sun fell on her flowing hair like light on a brown brook, and damp stones felt pleasantly cool beneath her bare feet. A cool wind came and blew around her cheeks. She closed her eyes for a moment, but the sudden creaking of a door made her open them again.

Gwynedd turned and saw Arvel, his arm in a sling, shut the heavy door and come towards her. There was a smile on his face, though he was pale and thin. "You should not have gotten up," Gwynedd said, smiling without a hint of sternness. She was not at all sorry to see him.

"Ah, well, that cannot be remedied now," Arvel said, laughing a little. He leaned over the wall beside Gwynedd and closed his eyes, exhaling as the wind whipped around his cheeks. His hair glinted in the sun.

Gwynedd glanced at him for a moment, her dark eyes softening, and then turned away. She looked down at the dark stones beneath her feet.

But her hair blew over the king's shoulder, and he turned to face her. "My Gwynedd," he said hoarsely, "I wish to be able to say those words without presumption. Do you–do you love me enough to say that you will be mine? I know that I love you enough—enough—ah, enough to do anything. I know that I do not deserve you, but I—I–" he shook his head, flushing, and laughed quietly at himself.

Gwynedd held out her hands, though they were shaking, and he took them. "I have hoped," he said, raising his eyes to meet hers.

She flushed, but she held his gaze and smiled. "I have loved you so long that I am ashamed to admit it."

Arvel smiled and laughed. Gwynedd loved his laugh, almost more than any other sound in the world. "Will you marry me, my Gwynedd?" the king said.

"Yes," Gwynedd said. No other words would come. They looked out over the hills, and though a gray cloud threatened to cover the sun, all the world they could see was golden.

Map Of Acorra

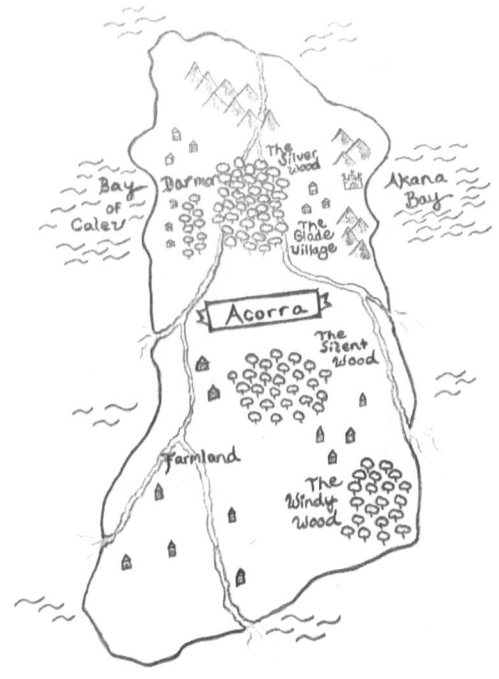

www.ingramcontent.com/pod-product-compliance
Lightning Source LLC
Chambersburg PA
CBHW050832180626
46814CB00004B/1589